2 D0461968

LEARNING THE RULES

Stephanie Perry Moore
&
Derrick Moore

LEARNING THE RULES

Alec London Series
Book 2

MOODY PUBLISHERS

CHICAGO

Edited by Kathryn Hall
Interior design: Ragont Design
Cover design: TS Design Studio
Cover images: TS Design Studio and 123rf.com

Library of Congress Cataloging-in-Publication Data

Moore, Stephanie Perry.
 Learning the rules / Stephanie Perry Moore and Derrick Moore.
    p. cm. -- (Alec London series ; bk. #2)
Summary: Ten-year-old Alec misses his mother when she decides to leave the family behind in Georgia while she goes to Los Angeles to work on a television show, is bullied when his older cousin moves in with his family, and gets picked on at school, but his troubles are eased when he decides to turn them over to God.
 ISBN 978-0-8024-0410-7
[1. Family problems--Fiction. 2. Bullies--Fiction. 3. Schools--Fiction. 4.Christian life--Fiction. 5. African Americans--Fiction.] I. Moore, Derrick C. II. Title.
 PZ7.M788125Le 2011
 [Fic]--dc22

                                2011010845

Printed by Bethany Press in Bloomington, MN - 01/2015

3 5 7 9 10 8 6 4 2

Printed in the United States of America

To our oldest daughter,
Sydni Derek Moore

We were overjoyed when we found
out you were finally on the way.
We wanted you so much, and we
prayed to be your parents.
We'll never forget when you were in the 4th grade.
Everything you learned back then gave
you a solid foundation to soar.
We know that if you—and every reader—
understand that life has rules
and follows them, you'll be dynamic!

Keep flying, Sydni . . . we love you!

Contents

MISTER
strong

1

"You're going back. You're not staying?" I said to my mom, trying to sound like the big, ten-year-old that I am. There's no way I could ever admit that I felt like a two-year-old on the inside.

"Oh, Alec. I wish you could understand," my mom said, coming over to me and placing her arms around my shoulders.

But I just kept huffing and puffing, until I couldn't hold back the tears any longer. I was thinking, *This isn't right. This isn't cool. This isn't fair. She cannot go back to California! She's home now, and this is where she needs to stay!*

Finally, I thought, *That's it! I simply refuse to let her go.* So, I stood up and said, "No! We need you here, Mom. Didn't you already do the pilot show? It was only supposed to be for a little while. Remember?"

Antoine couldn't even look at Mom. His back was

turned to her, and his arms were folded. As much as I knew how badly he wanted to be tough, this had to be tough for him on the inside too.

We just had the best Thanksgiving ever when we were all together having dinner at my friend Morgan's house. Mom had come home and surprised us at the last minute. She'd been gone for a couple of months. Now, only a day later, she was leaving again.

Mom was a TV star when she was a child. But her dream time was over. Now she needed to be a mother to Antoine and me, and a wife to Dad. If no one else would fight for her to stay, then I was gonna be the one to stand up to her.

So I tried again. "I cannot let you go back, Mom. I'm sorry. No," I told her with all the strength I could pull together.

"Andre! Talk to him," Mom said to Dad, as if he was on her side.

She couldn't have been thinking that her leaving was gonna be okay. She had no idea of how it felt to have all of us crying every night for two months while she was away. There was no way Dad could let her do this to us again.

I watched Mom whisper something in his ear. He tugged away from her, and said, "Lisa, seriously. I have to deal with these boys when you're not here. Yeah, we're excited that you came home, but all of a sudden you're ready to leave again. What did you expect to happen? What are you thinking?"

"We start shooting again tomorrow. The show got picked up, and we're getting ready to make eight episodes. There's no guarantee how long it will last, but for now we're going to be on a local network right here in Atlanta. So, who knows? Maybe I won't be in California for a long time. I just need you guys to understand."

What was there to understand? We were in shock and hurting bad. It was a feeling worse than waking up on Christmas morning and finding no presents under the tree. Our mom was chasing her dreams and our dreams were turning into nightmares.

I walked over to Dad and said, "You have to stop her. You've gotta tell her we need her. Don't let her walk out the door, Dad. Please!"

Antoine couldn't take it any longer. He turned around and said to me, "Quit bein' a baby. If she has to leave, then let her. We can't force her to stay."

"Antoine!" Mom called his name as if she was shocked at what he just said.

Antoine just looked at her sadly.

"Antoine," Mom repeated again, this time with her head hanging low.

"You know what? Go to your room, son," Dad stepped in between them and told him. He didn't want Antoine to hurt her feelings even more.

Mom's eyes were filled with tears, just like mine. I wanted to wipe her tears away. I didn't want her to hurt, but she was definitely hurting us. All we wanted was for her to stay with us. But she wasn't trying to do or hear that. She was ready to go.

"Alec, honey," she said, touching my face and bending down to kiss me on my cheek. "I love you guys so much. I'm sorry if this seems really hard, but that is not my intent. I'm already helping so much more with the extra money that's coming in. If the show becomes a hit—"

"What? You can be a big star? Without a family, what does that matter, Mom?" I asked her.

I was sounding harsh, and I didn't like it. I was acting more like Antoine, knowing I shouldn't have been talking to Mom like that. Even so, I wanted to be honest because I know that holding things in isn't good either. There were so many nights that I just wanted to tell her how I felt so she could feel the same hurt.

"Do I need to take you to the airport?" Dad spoke up and asked her.

"Dad!"

"Son, let me do this. Okay? Your mom is set on going."

My father has a strong voice. Even though he was willing to help Mom leave us again, Dad wanted her to stay just as much as we did. He was putting on a huge front just like Antoine. Like father, like son, I guess.

"I'm sorry," Mom whispered to him.

"If you were sorry, you would realize what you're doing to all of us," Dad told her.

"Don't go there with me, Andre. I finally have my chance. I can't turn my back on this opportunity. You remember all those shows I auditioned for? Well finally I get a big part, and our show is getting picked up to air on cable TV. I told you how much I really love my character. Besides, we all know this won't last forever."

"Yeah, I read the script. It's about a mom holding down her family. But, guess what? Have you thought about what's happening in your real life?" Dad asked her. Then, without giving her a chance to say anything, he said, "Never mind, you don't have to answer that. Lisa, you're gonna have to think about what you're doing to this family. I don't know if we can put up with this much longer."

Mom acted like she didn't know how to answer Dad. She just nodded and reached out to hug me again. My arms were so numb I couldn't even move. She squeezed me tight and let me go.

Dad looked at me and said, "Son, I'm taking your mom to the airport. Go on upstairs and let Antoine know that I'll be back as soon as I can."

A few minutes later, I heard the front door close. Just like that, Mom was gone again, and I was heartbroken again.

● ● ●

"Alec, wake up. I let you sleep late, but now it's time to get up," I heard Dad say.

It was the Saturday after Thanksgiving Day. Mom had been gone a whole twenty-four hours, and Grandma was still away visiting her sister. Since there were no ladies in the house, Dad, Antoine, and I kept to ourselves. We even fixed our own food and ate when we felt like it. We were sulking in our own way and just trying to deal with life.

Then Dad told us, "Your grandmother will be back soon, and we need to clean up this house."

I grunted, "Dad, I stayed in my room all day yesterday. If anybody messed up the house, it must have been Antoine."

"Nuh-uh, Dad. I didn't do it," Antoine told him, while pointing at me. "Alec was the one who messed it up."

He didn't give me a chance to say anything else. Before he walked away, Dad said, "I don't care who did it. We're all going to clean it up."

As soon as Dad couldn't see me, I stomped into the bathroom to wash my face. There was a pile of Antoine's clothes on the floor. Toothpaste from his tube was all over the sink. And I had to clean up after him? Ugh! I was so angry that I didn't even feel like arguing with Antoine about it. I just did it.

After I finished cleaning up that mess, I joined Dad and Antoine to straighten up the rest of the house. Suddenly, we heard a voice call out.

"Where's my grandbabies?"

Running to hug her first, I said, "I'm right here, Grandma. Boy, did I miss you."

I felt a squeeze in return, but when I looked up, I saw that I had hugged the wrong lady. For a minute, I was confused. The two ladies standing in front of me looked like twins.

My mouth hung open as I heard Grandma say, "Alec, I'm over here, baby. That's my sister, Dot."

I was still standing there, not sure what to say to either one of them. "I know, I know," Grandma said when she saw my face. "Everybody thinks we're the same person . . . happens all the time . . . and she's three years older than me," she said with a chuckle.

"Come here, boy. You can still give me a hug. I'm your Aunt Dot," she said, reaching for me.

"Antoine, where are you, boy?" Grandma called out.

"He's finishing up cleaning his room," I said.

"Antoine, get down here!" Dad called.

As soon as Antoine ran down the stairs, we were both looking at a boy who had just stepped through the door. With a basketball in his hands, I thought for a minute that he was an NBA player. Next to me and my brother, this guy looked like a giant.

"This is my grandson, Lil Pete," Aunt Dot said to Antoine, Dad, and me.

"Hello, son. It's good to meet you," Dad said right away, as he held out his hand. The boy ignored him and acted like he didn't know that Dad wanted to shake his hand.

"Young man, remember your manners. I expect you to show some respect," Dad said to Lil Pete.

"Sorry," Lil Pete grunted, as he stuck out his hand to Dad.

"Hi," Antoine and I both said at the same time.

"Hey, I'm Lil P.," the boy said with a lot of attitude. I guess he wanted us to know that he was the coolest kid around. Then, without any warning, he said, "Catch," as he tossed the basketball to Antoine.

I knew Dad wouldn't allow that, but before he could say a word, Grandma said, "Now, I won't have no tossin' balls in here. Y'all need to go outside with that."

When the grown-ups all headed toward the kitchen, there we were, alone with Lil P. Antoine and I both looked at each other like we didn't wanna play with this big kid.

Lil P. didn't waste any time before he came over to Antoine and put his head in a headlock. It wasn't real tight, but just enough to scare my brother and me. It was working too. When we got outside to play, Lil P. kept shoving me every time I got the ball. He wasn't playing by any rules.

"Y'all are some wimps! What? You can't handle me?" Lil P. said, as he darted between us.

"Man, you're like a high schooler out here tryin' to play with some kids," Antoine told him.

"Whatever. I'm just in the seventh grade," said Lil P.

I swallowed hard when I heard that. *If this guy is only in the seventh grade, then I must be in kindergarten,* I thought. He was huge.

Antoine stood up to him. "Why do you have to be so rough? Shovin' people and pushin' them down isn't cool, man. You gotta know the rules of basketball, so play the right way. If not, you can play by yourself."

My brother started to walk away, and I was right behind him.

"Wait. Come on back," Lil P. said with a laugh. "I'm only jokin'. Y'all live in your big old house. Your grandma cooks and cleans for you. But y'all need to loosen up some."

"You live with your grandma, too," I said to him.

"Yeah, but that don't make me a wimp."

I looked at Antoine, and Antoine looked at me. We both looked at him. Lil P. had muscles. He was right; he looked like a tough dude.

"On my block, we play street ball. If you wanna win, then you gotta have an edge. If you wanna be the man on the court, then basketball's gotta be physical."

"Well, you do have some smooth moves," Antoine said, as we watched Lil P. spin around, jump up in the air, and try to dunk.

He wasn't embarrassed by missing that shot. Lil P. acted real cool and said, "I'm workin' on that."

Hoping to put him in check, I had to say something. So I told him, "I'm not tryin' to play with people who wanna hurt other people."

"I ain't tryin' to hurt nobody. If you don't wanna play, then don't," Lil P. replied.

"Okay. You be the referee," Antoine jumped in and said. "I'm not scared of him. Let's go. I can get rough if I want to. Let's play, cuz."

I couldn't believe Lil P.'s big talk was working on

Antoine. My brother could easily be pulled in by a challenge and didn't know when to back down. He was always trying to show people he wasn't scared.

I just prayed, *"Lord, please don't let my brother get hurt. I know Lil P. is our cousin, but we don't know him. He looks so tough. Be with Antoine. Amen."*

As I watched them play, Antoine seemed to be holding his own. When he got pushed, he pushed back. Antoine didn't know how to dunk yet, but he was shooting 3s and Lil P. was getting mad. When my brother beat him in a game of 21, it pushed Lil P. over the edge. He really wanted to show us that he was in charge.

"All right, all right," my cousin said to Antoine. "That's how you play. Don't let nobody push you around. Hold your ground and play hard!"

Lil P. got so sure of himself that he started to put on a big show. It was clear to me that he couldn't rap or dance, but no one could tell him that he wasn't jammin'. He was offbeat and wasn't even rhyming, but he kept acting like he was a star. Then it got really bad when Lil P. started using bad words and Antoine followed him. I couldn't believe my brother was going right along with him.

My cousin had better watch out, because if Dad heard what Lil P. was saying, then he wouldn't be allowed at our house anymore. Lil P. didn't have to worry; I wasn't gonna tell on him. But I wasn't gonna follow a guy that I knew was wrong either.

● ● ●

"Look at that new kid. Man, he's at the wrong school, ain't he?" Tyrod said, as he joked about the new boy. The rest of the class turned toward the door, as Mr. Wade walked in with a new student.

I had to admit. The kid did seem a little out of place. Not only was he white and everyone else in the class was black, he had red-orange hair and blue eyes. On top of that, he was wearing cowboy boots. Tyrod was having a field day teasing him.

He said to the boy, "Looks like you need to go back to the rodeo where you belong."

"Why don't you hush?" Morgan said. "Nobody wants to hear that."

"Then why don't you close your ears, Miss Goody-Two-Shoes? Nobody was talkin' to you anyway."

Mr. Wade brought the new student to the front of the class and introduced him. "Everyone, this is Gilmer Luck."

"Gilmer Luck. That's a weird name," Tyrod called out.

"Young man, that's enough," said Mr. Wade, frowning at Tyrod.

Mr. Wade went on to tell our class that Gilmer was from Tennessee. He and his mom had recently moved to Georgia. I watched Gilmer as he looked around the class. It didn't seem to bother him that we all looked different from him.

From the look on his face, he didn't seem to wanna get to know any of us either. That was cool with me since I had enough friends. In fact, I could relate to how he felt. When

I first came to this school, I wasn't looking for new buddies either.

Mr. Wade pointed out the empty seat right in front of me. Just as Gilmer walked toward me to sit down, I lifted up my head as if to say, "What's up?" He just sat down and didn't pay me any attention. I didn't care, but I thought he was acting a little rude. He didn't have to show me twice. I wasn't gonna beg anybody to be their friend.

Mr. Wade began by teaching a lesson on measurements. Although we learned something about gallons, pints, and quarts in the third grade, he was giving us more information. I think most of us were confused. When he asked us to pair up in groups of two, it didn't matter if my partner was Trey or Morgan. I just didn't wanna pair up with Gilmer.

Trey came over and surprised me by saying, "I'll partner with the new kid. You work with Morgan."

"You wanna pair with Gilmer?" I asked him.

"Yeah, he seems cool."

"Fine by me."

I got up and went over to Morgan's desk, and we started working out the problems on the chart Mr. Wade passed out.

After fifteen minutes, I was so glad when Mr. Wade said to put down our pencils. It was time for P.E. Those measurement problems were getting really tough.

Coach Jones was super cool. He made learning all kinds of sports fun. He knew how to make his students laugh and how to push them to do their best.

This was the time for us to compete in the Presidential Academy. It's a national physical exercise program, and the top scorers get awards.

I ran the fastest time in the 40-yard dash. I did the most sit-ups. And I also made the longest long jump. But when it came to the test for running the mile, the new student, Gilmer, beat me. He was better than all the rest of us. I could run short distances okay, but long distances made me gasp for air.

While I was bent over trying to catch my breath, Trey leaned down and said, "You need to get to know him. Make him feel welcome, and maybe he can help you run the mile better. It must feel pretty scary being the only white kid in the class."

"What?" I said completely annoyed. "No way. I'm not gettin' to know anybody. You worked with him on the math problems. That's enough for me."

"Yeah, but he barely said a word."

"See, that should tell you something," Morgan said, joining our conversation. "If he didn't wanna talk, then maybe he's going through something with his family. Mr. Wade did say he moved here with his mom. What happened to his dad? I'm with Trey. He does need a friend or two."

Trey smiled and said, "That's exactly why he needs us. We're like the Three Musketeers. We can help anybody."

"I don't want to be rude or anything, but I do have my issues with making friends," Morgan said. She was looking at the girls on the other side of the room.

"Forget about them," Trey told her. "It can be me, you, Alec, and Gilmer."

Hearing her say that, I asked Morgan, "What's goin' on with you and those girls?"

"Just forget about it," she said, holding her head down.

"She's upset because they don't wanna be her friend. The girls in our class are mean," said Trey.

I felt sorry for her. Morgan is a really cool girl, and I didn't understand why the other girls didn't like her.

Turning back to dealing with Gilmer, I said, "If you wanna be his friend, Trey, then go ahead and talk to him. Just leave me out of it."

When Trey walked off, I looked over at the girls in our class. They were laughing and joking together. I said to Morgan, "It's their problem if they don't wanna be friends with you."

Last year in our class, Morgan had two girlfriends who followed her every move. I wasn't trying to fix the world, but I wasn't trying to let my friend be sad either. It made me want to think of something that could help her.

We sat on a bench and watched Trey as he went up to Gilmer. He was talking, but Gilmer was pretty much ignoring him. Trey wouldn't stop trying though. He definitely had his mind made up that he was gonna make friends with Gilmer.

All of a sudden, Gilmer burst out and said, "What don't you get? I told you to leave me alone. I don't want to be your friend. I don't want to be anyone's friend. Go away!"

Trey was about to open his mouth and say something back. He didn't like that Gilmer got loud with him. But by that time Morgan and I had rushed over and pulled him away. The situation didn't need to get any worse than it was.

Trey was a little shook up. He said, "I don't know what to say. He didn't have to go off on me like that. I'm just tryin' to hang out with him."

"Why?" I asked.

"Probably because of what I learned from you, Alec. When you came here in the second grade, you were mean and tough. After a while, I found out it was because you had some things going on at home. If I had taken the time to get to know you at the beginning, we would've been friends just like that," Trey said, snapping his fingers.

Then, in a proud voice, he added, "I turned a tough guy into my best buddy one time, and I can do it again."

"Okay, like Morgan said, he might need you. But now must not be the time," I replied.

"I get that. Even so, something serious is going on with that guy. He needs me. He needs us. I see him acting all tough like he's fine being alone. But he's not Mister Strong."

Letter to Mom

Dear Mom,

Please forgive me for saying so, but it feels so much like you are neglecting your family. I don't mean to sound harsh, but this is really hard. Now that you have a chance for a new role, I know you want to follow your dream of being a TV star. But you know what? If it means you have to be away from us, then I don't want you to take it.

Mom, we met our cousin, Lil Pete. He likes to call himself Lil P., and Antoine thinks he's great. He's older and much bigger than me and Antoine. This guy tries to be so rough on the basketball court. And he uses bad words too. He is not a good role model. But I'm not afraid of him.

We've got a new kid named Gilmer at school. He's the only white student in our class. Trey wanted to make him feel welcome, but Tyrod joked about his clothes. Gilmer didn't fight back, he just stayed to himself.

Mom, I do want you to be happy, I just miss you so much. Please come home soon.

> Your son,
> Trying to be Strong Alec

Word Search: Basketball Terms

At any basketball game—little league, middle school, high school, college, or pros—the terms below are often used.

```
U  E  G  V  L  T  X  A  V  F  J  N
T  O  J  E  X  C  I  T  I  N  G  B
L  H  E  H  K  M  K  V  Y  O  B  C
G  Z  R  P  U  X  N  F  J  F  F  O
N  K  S  E  X  F  B  U  S  R  J  M
I  N  E  C  E  J  M  N  E  K  P  P
L  U  Y  I  I  P  E  E  K  A  X  E
B  D  S  Y  B  A  T  Q  S  W  X  T
B  M  W  A  K  H  R  S  A  U  G  I
I  A  L  E  R  F  Y  W  H  Y  I  N
R  L  R  O  A  I  H  E  M  O  T  G
D  S  W  Y  O  N  L  F  P  E  T  E
```

FREETHROW (Free Throw)   **JERSEY**   **JUMPBALL (Jump Ball)**
PASS   **SLAMDUNK (Slam Dunk)**
SNEAKERS   **THREEPTSHOT (Three-Point Shot)**

TOUGHEN UP

2

It was time for season tryouts for the basketball team. Because of my age, I had to move up a division. I was a little nervous about it. Probably because I could see that these guys were much bigger than me. On the football field when we all wear pads and helmets, I'm much closer to their size.

"Watch how it's done, little brother," Antoine said. Before running out onto the court, he elbowed me in the arm a couple times.

"Alec, get on out there!" said Coach Williams, our basketball instructor. "I still have to pick my starting lineup."

I looked back at him as if to say, *"It's not going to be me!"*

It wasn't that I didn't have confidence. I just knew from watching the other players, the older boys had been training longer than me. I looked lost out there. They were taller and could get the layups easier. They were older and had more practice at hitting free throws. Three-point shots came easy to them because their arms were longer. They could jump and grab the rebounds.

There were a couple of guys I knew from the football team. Jelani was our quarterback, and Miles was our offensive lineman. Jelani and I were cool with each other. We got along good during football season. He told me that he wanted the ball because he wanted to be a starter. So, as soon as the ball got to my hands and he was open, I tossed it to him.

But Antoine was acting way too aggressive. He not only knocked the ball away from him, he knocked Jelani down real hard. Jelani fell on his face, covering his nose.

"Ow, ow!! I'm hurt! That wasn't fair! That wasn't right!"

"Aw, quit whinin'," Antoine said, as if he didn't care that our teammate was in pain.

"Let's go! Let's go!" yelled Coach Williams.

But Jelani wasn't getting up. Antoine leaned over him and said, "You need to get up and quit tryin' to get me in trouble. We're just playin' ball!"

Jelani wouldn't look at my brother. I stood there watching the scene, hoping that his nose wasn't broken. When some of the boys shouted for Coach Williams to come, Antoine came over and stood next to me. He pinched my arm to get my attention, but I didn't say anything. I just looked at him like he was crazy. Quickly, I moved away from him. Then he came and stood beside me again. This time, he was mumbling something.

"What?" I asked him, letting him know that I wasn't playing with him.

But he still wouldn't come out and say what he wanted. He just kept moving his mouth without saying any words, as if I could read his lips.

Coach Williams asked, "All right. What happened here?"

"He hit me! He hit me, Coach!" Jelani rolled over and there was red blood gushing out of his nose like ketchup squeezing from a bottle.

Coach Williams yelled, "Miles, go and get some paper towels. Jelani, calm down. You're going to be okay. Tell me what happened."

"He hit me! He hit me!" Jelani kept saying and pointing at Antoine.

"I didn't hit him, Coach!" Antoine defended himself. "We were just playin' a little ball. I was just showin' him how to do some moves. You know, bein' aggressive like you said, Coach. I went out there to make somethin' happen. I wasn't too rough. He's just a wimp! Tell him, Alec!"

I just shook my head. I couldn't believe he wanted me to agree with what he just said. Didn't he realize I saw the whole thing? Antoine did hit Jelani real hard. He meant to knock him down and hurt him. And I knew exactly where he got the idea from—our cousin, Lil P.

Miles came back with some paper towels. Coach

helped Jelani to his feet, trying to stop his nosebleed.

"You're going to be okay. You're going to be okay. Alec, you saw it, right?" asked Coach.

I wanted to tell the truth, but I knew if I said I saw it then he'd asked me what I saw. And I didn't want to have to tell him that I saw my brother doing something really wrong. Either way, I had no choice.

Because I knew the difference between right and wrong, I said, "Yes, sir."

Before he said anything else, I turned to walk away. Putting my hands on my head, I just prayed, *"Lord, this is a hot mess, as Grandma would say. Help!"*

"Alec, you have to tell me what happened."

"Yeah, Alec! Tell him! Tell him!" Antoine said. He just knew I was going to back him up.

And I almost did, until I looked at Jelani with blood all over his face and shirt. I knew Antoine was wrong.

In my softest voice, I said, "My brother was a little hard with him."

"You hear that! See, Coach! Told you! He did this on purpose." Jelani started charging over to Antoine, but the coach stood between both of them.

"Jelani, sit down so that nosebleed can stop!"

"Antoine, I'm tempted to put you off the team. Go over there and sit down. I'm going to call your dad this afternoon."

Antoine went over to the bleachers, but he didn't sit down. He started kicking at the air. Then he hit the bleacher. He was shouting. It was bad.

I rushed over to my brother as fast as I could. "Why are you making this worse?" I asked him.

Antoine growled like a hungry grizzly bear, "You'd better get out of my face. You think I hit him? See what you're gonna get at home when I slug you!"

"Whatever," I sighed, not happy he was threatening me. "I don't *think* you hit him. I *know* you hit him. You know you did too."

"What I know is that my brother is always supposed to have my back. But I know you're jealous that I'm gettin' a chance to start. You're just a little boy who's tryin' to take my spot away from me again. It's just not fair."

"You hurting people so you can stay in the starting lineup isn't fair either."

"What do you care? You're not the coach!"

"Fine, Antoine, go ahead and think your mean actions are right."

"I know it was right. You'd better watch your back, bro. You don't have mine, I won't have yours."

"Ooh, I'm scared," I said to him, sorry that we hadn't squashed all the tension that was between us for good.

Earlier in the year, we had trouble getting along. Then we moved past all that. At least, I thought we did. However, when I jogged back onto the court and Coach tossed me the ball, I looked over at my brother and practically saw steam shooting from his ears like a train's engine. But you know where he was mad? On the bench, that's where. Now he

31

had to really think about that. Threatening me? What was Antoine thinking? He was acting like a baby. Ugh!

● ● ●

It's here! It's time for the Christmas party! I was so excited to get to school. I couldn't wait to give my gifts to my two good friends. I had a necklace for Morgan and a watch for Trey. As soon as Trey saw me, he dashed over to my desk.

He saw the two gifts sitting in front of me. "Aw, look! Both of these are for me," Trey said with a silly smile on his face.

"Only one of them, dude. Here you go," I said, handing him a box wrapped in red Christmas paper.

"You shouldn't have. I didn't get anything for you," he said, trying to sound like a girl.

"Whatever, dude. I didn't get this for you just so you could get me something," I said. It felt good that I got him something just because.

"Aw! See, you're so cool. I'm just playin'. I did get you somethin'," Trey said, as he pulled out a real large, gift-wrapped box from underneath his desk.

"Trey and Alec sitting in a tree . . . " Tyrod started singing.

Trey got real mad, but I said, "Whatever. Don't even sweat it. It's not like anybody got him a gift. He doesn't have any real friends. He's just jealous."

Tyrod heard me and grunted before storming off to his

seat. He wasn't going to get under my skin. Trey grinned once he realized I was right. Then the two of us had fun checking out our gifts.

When I opened mine, it was an autographed football of all the Falcon players and a framed picture of me with the starting running back. Tyrod looked green with envy.

"Wow!" I said. "Hey, man, thanks. This is great."

After I saw what Trey got me, I didn't want him to open his. I didn't think he would like my little gift, but he said that he always wanted a sports watch. Now he'd be able to set his alarm and get himself up in the morning.

Trey was cooler with me than my own brother. Although we weren't just alike, I appreciated him for who he was.

Then he saw me look down at the other gift that I had for Morgan.

"She's not gonna want to talk to you," Trey said to me. As I was listening to him, I saw Morgan's sad face as she quickly left the room.

I frowned and asked him, "Why? What's wrong?"

"Shavon and Lacy have been acting really mean to her."

Those two girls thought they were all that. They weren't better than Morgan, but they were always trying to make her feel like they were. They wouldn't let her in their little circle and made Morgan think that she wasn't pretty enough. I knew it was getting to Morgan, but I didn't know that she was taking it so hard.

We had a few more minutes before the bell, so I headed out to the hallway and went down by the girls' washroom. I waited for Morgan to come out. When she did, her face looked all puffy.

"Hi. I got you something," I said, not knowing what else to say.

Reaching for the little box, she said, "Thanks. Your gift is at my house. I couldn't bring it to school because it's too big."

"You didn't have to get me anything," I said to her.

"You're my friend. That's what friends do."

"Okay," I replied.

Then she tried to walk away from me.

"Wait, Morgan. I waited for you because I want to talk to you. Don't do me like that." Just as I said that, I saw some fifth grade boys looking at me like I was silly or something.

"What's wrong? Talk to me. Please."

She held her head down, as her eyes started to water again. The last thing I wanted to do was see her cry. I had no intentions of getting into a fight with anybody. But, if they're making Morgan cry, I'm gonna have to talk to Shavon and Lacy and get them straight.

"Where are they?"

"Where are who?" Morgan said, wiping away her tears.

"Shavon and Lacy. I know they made you get all sad and stuff. It's the last day before Christmas break. You shouldn't be unhappy. We should be having a good time. We won't have any schoolwork today. We'll be playing games, watching movies, and having a party. I mean, you can hang with me. Forget them."

"I appreciate that, Alec, but don't you understand? I'm not a boy. You and Trey are great, and I do have my girlfriends from last year. I hang out with them on the weekends. But school isn't fun when you don't fit in. That's why I wanna fit in with the other girls. Please leave me alone. You wouldn't understand," Morgan said, walking away.

I caught up to her and said, "Look, if being their friend is what you want, then let's pray about it. And after we do, we need to just leave it alone. We can't change people—but God can. If those girls aren't nice enough to appreciate you, then be strong enough to stand alone. Hang out with me and Trey until God brings you someone else."

"Wow," Morgan said, wiping her face again. "Look at what God's done for you!"

"I guess He's helping me grow . . . I don't know."

"Okay. Pray for me."

"Right here?" I was still watching those fifth grade boys who were hanging out in the hall.

"Why not? You can't be ashamed."

Quickly, I replied, "I'm not ashamed."

"Then pray for me right here."

She grabbed my hand, and I almost wanted to pull it away. But I squeezed it tight and prayed, "Lord, please bless Morgan. Amen."

She smiled and said, "Thank you, Alec." It seemed like she felt a little better.

When we got to the classroom, Tyrod was talking all loud with some kids standing around him. When Morgan and I got a little closer, we saw that he was picking on Gilmer again.

"You need to get some Nikes for Christmas . . . those tacky cowboy boots you've got on are like the ones people wore in old western movies. And, man, that hair . . . do you ever comb it? Do you wash it in mud? It looks like dirt is all in your hair."

"This is crazy. Why won't Tyrod just leave him alone?" asked Morgan.

Then Shavon and Lacy started laughing and picking on Gilmer too. They were pointing at his clothes and said they made him look like a homeless person.

"And you want to be good friends with them?" I asked Morgan.

Morgan looked at the girls and shook her head. "I think you're right. God does know best."

Then I looked at Gilmer. He wasn't trying to get away from the joking, and he didn't seem upset by it either. It was like he had a shield around him and none of what they were saying was bothering him at all. He wasn't dumb. Gilmer had been making all As since he came to our class.

When Mr. Wade came into the room, he let us know if we didn't settle down there wasn't going to be a party. Gilmer never opened his mouth to say, "They're picking on me." Or, "Please tell them to stop." He just stayed calm and kept reading his comic book. I really sort of admired that he had such thick skin.

● ● ●

I couldn't believe it! I was actually on an airplane headed to California to spend the holidays with Mom. Over Christmas break, Antoine got invited to play in a basketball tournament with a travel team. So, he and Dad were on their way to Orlando.

When Mom first asked me if I wanted to visit her or stay with Grandma, I quickly jumped at the chance to be with my mother. In a flash, I said yes so fast that it felt like I was making a slam dunk.

Mom made sure the airline knew that I was traveling alone so that they would be looking out for me. Since she let them know that I am a minor, every few minutes the flight attendant would come and ask me, "Mr. London, are you okay?"

After about the tenth time, I finally said, "Ma'am, can you please call me Alec? I'm not that old."

The lady replied with a smile, "Sure, but when I say 'Mr. London' that just means I'm giving you respect." Then rubbing my head, she added, "You're so adorable."

Before she walked away, this really nice lady pinched my cheek. I didn't want her to think that I was a baby, but I didn't mind all the attention either. She made sure I had everything I wanted and wasn't nervous about the trip. How cool was that?

When it was time for us to land, the plane started dipping and I could feel us dropping down a bit. My stomach felt a little uneasy like it did when I rode on one of those roller coasters at an amusement park.

The flight attendant came to get everybody ready to land. When she saw that I was uncomfortable, she smiled at me and said, "Are you okay?" I nodded. Then she told me to put up my tray and relax. I'm a big boy, and I'm tough. I kept my mind on how happy I would be to see my mom. So, even when my ears started popping, I could handle it.

As soon as I got off the plane and stepped into the waiting area, I saw her. She was the prettiest woman in the whole airport. With a grin wider than I imagined the Pacific Ocean to be, Mom called out my name.

"Alec! I'm right here," she shouted, as she bounced up and down, waving at me.

I rushed to her arms and hugged her so tight. I was so glad to be with her. And although it had only been a month since I last saw her—I missed her so much.

"Look at you!" she said, "You look taller than you were at Thanksgiving," she said, as she hugged me really tight.

I didn't want to answer, and I didn't want to let go of her hand. I just wanted to be with my mom—and I was. It was a great feeling.

After we claimed my bag, she led me out of the airport to the parking lot. As soon as we got in the car, she said, "I'm so glad you're here, Alec. My show is going really well. I'm excited for you to meet some of my cast members and crew. My producer, Kim, can't wait to meet you. The three of us are going out to dinner later on this evening, but for now it's just you and me. And I'm going to show you Hollywood!"

Mom didn't know it, but I already had the best view of all. Hollywood is a shining star only because she is here. Mom didn't know that I came on a mission. I didn't want to like Hollywood too much. I was there to talk my mother into coming home. If Antoine wasn't going to say it, if Dad wasn't going to say it, then I'd be the one to keep it real. My plan was to make her want to move back home.

I'm glad things were going well for Mom. And I couldn't wait to meet her friend Kim. But none of the people she worked with were her family. They couldn't give her the love and care that only Dad, Antoine, and I could.

We drove around the city, and Mom showed me lots of interesting things. I saw the huge letters with the word H-O-L-L-Y-W-O-O-D spelled out in the mountain. We walked down the streets where the names of Hollywood stars cover the ground. Then we drove by the Staples Center and I saw where the Lakers play ball.

"This is so cool! The Lakers play here!" I said, unable to hold back my excitement.

"Yep, and I have a surprise for you. Kim and I are going to take you there tonight. You're going to love it!"

"For real, Mom? We're going to the game! Oh, yeah!"

"See, I knew you'd like L.A."

Then I caught myself. "I mean, going to the game is okay," I said, changing my tone.

She reached over and patted my forehead, "Don't play with me. I know how much you like the Lakers."

When we got to her place, it was really nice. The only thing was the size. It was too small. The whole place was one big room that Mom called a studio apartment. She told me that her bed was in the wall and I was going to sleep on the couch.

In one corner there was a small dining area, and I noticed a gold box lying on the table. When I saw that the nice box had my name on it, I said, "I guess I can't open it until Christmas, huh?"

She picked it up and handed it to me. "No, it's from my friend Kim. You can open it right now," Mom told me.

As quickly as I could, I tore off the wrapping paper to find a cool Lakers jersey. I was too excited. "Wow! Mom! Wow! This is great! I can't wait to thank your friend!"

"Well, go ahead and put it on. I'm going to brush my teeth and freshen up so we'll be ready when Kim comes."

The doorbell rang while Mom was in the bathroom, and she told me to answer it. To my surprise, when I opened the door, some guy was standing there looking at me.

"Are you Alec?" he asked.

"Yeah," I said, having no clue of who this man was. *How come he knows my name?* I thought.

"I'm Kim, your mom's producer. I'm here to take you

guys to the game. Man, you look nice in that jersey. Can I come in?"

The guy was sounding real smooth. I just stood there looking at him from head to toe. Kim was a guy? Mom's friend is a guy? Quickly, I decided that I didn't like this one bit. I didn't want him to come in. I didn't want the jersey. I didn't want him to be my mom's friend.

I couldn't move, so I was still standing in the doorway when Mom came out of the bathroom. She sounded a little too excited when she said, "Hey, Kim! We're ready to go. I see you met Alec. Alec, Kim is the producer of my show, and he's volunteered to be our tour guide for the time you're here with me. Isn't that nice of him?"

I just stood there and didn't say anything. I couldn't say anything.

"Alec! Move over and let Kim in, son," she said with a light laugh, seeing that I wasn't going to move out of the way.

There wasn't much privacy in her studio place, but I got up close to my mom. I looked at her with my hands up as if to say, *"What's up? I'm not sure about this."* Mom gave me a look and said "Sorry I didn't tell you Kim was a guy, but don't worry, everything is okay."

It didn't matter what she might try to tell me, this was a disaster. Why didn't she tell me that Kim was a man? I didn't say a word in the car or at the basketball game. I was at a Lakers' game, one of my favorite NBA teams, and I couldn't even enjoy it. I just kept looking at my mom, laughing and having fun with this Kim guy. This was not fun for me.

Then when Mom went to the washroom, he leaned over to me and said, "Your mom is cool. She's really cool."

"Yeah, my dad thinks so too . . . and so do my brother and I."

"Well, I'm out here with her in L.A," he said, giving me a wink.

"Sometimes all our hopes and dreams don't work out, ya know? We just gotta be open to new things. Your mom is a great lady," he said, rubbing my head.

There were so many things I wanted to say to Kim, but just then Mom came back. I looked at him in a very mean way and he winked at me again. Then they went back to laughing.

Before I left Hollywood, I knew I was gonna have to talk to her about all this. It might not be easy, but I had to just share my heart and put it all out there. This was a call for me to toughen up.

Letter to Mom

Dear Mom,

I know you were shocked to find out about the stunt Antoine pulled on the basketball court. He was way too rough and knocked down a boy named Jelani real hard. Mom, Antoine did it on purpose, and Jelani panicked. He was really scared.

Antoine was trying to be like Lil P. I didn't want to tell on my brother, but since you taught me right from wrong, I had to tell the coach what really happened.

Mom, you and Dad have always told me to tell the truth. But I feel bad that Antoine doesn't understand why I had to do the right thing. Now we have a major problem between us.

I'm happy to be in Hollywood. But there is something we need to talk about. I feel like I can handle tough stuff. We'll see if I'm really ready.

Your son,
Trying to be Tough Alec

Word Search: Basketball Positions

Every team must have 5 players on the court at all times. Also, for organized basketball there probably are two other important roles. Here are some of the great positions in the game of basketball.

```
S  M  A  L  L  F  O  R  W  A  R  D
C  P  N  H  Z  N  E  G  N  X  R  R
H  W  O  O  C  F  L  U  X  A  I  A
A  V  M  I  E  A  X  H  W  X  N  U
M  Y  B  R  N  L  O  R  P  H  S  G
P  J  E  R  G  T  O  C  F  O  U  T
I  E  J  R  S  F  G  W  Y  O  B  O
O  M  T  E  R  W  D  U  N  P  C  O
N  V  R  E  K  N  I  C  A  S  K  H
S  Z  W  L  O  O  H  C  S  R  C  S
D  O  T  I  P  M  S  P  T  Q  D  A
P  R  R  E  T  N  E  C  I  W  G  U
```

CENTER   COACH   POINTGUARD (Point Guard)

POWERFORWARD (Power Forward)   REFEREE

SHOOTGUARD (Shooting Guard)   SMALLFORWARD (Small Forward)

GOOD
lesson

3

Mom just kept going on and on about all the plans she and Kim had for us to spend New Year's Eve together. It was bad enough that I had to spend Christmas with her friend. He had no problem letting me know that he thought my mom was super special.

As I looked at her across the small apartment, I could understand why. She was beautiful. Her hair bounced and swayed whenever she moved. She was always smiling, and she loved to give out hugs.

But she was taken, and I wanted this man to know that. Somehow, someway, I was gonna have to tell her that I didn't want to hang out anymore with Mr. Kim, the big-time producer.

"Alec, did you hear me, honey? I have the day all planned out. After breakfast, I want to show you some more sights. In the afternoon, we're going to take you bowling. Then tonight, we'll end up with dinner at a comedy club that has a funny show for kids your age. It's going to be so much fun!"

None of that sounded exciting to me. So, I just sank down on the couch. What really bothered me was that she didn't even mention Dad a lot. She talked about Antoine all the time, wishing he was out here too and asking me what he's been up to. But she didn't seem to care that much about what's happening with Dad—and that was a problem for me.

Mom noticed that my mood wasn't so happy. "Okay," she said, coming to sit beside me on the couch. "Talk to me, Alec. What's going on? You've got a long face, and it's New Year's Eve. You should be excited because we're together. I know you're leaving tomorrow, but can we enjoy the day with no more long faces. Please?"

I just looked at her for a moment. I mean, I'm her ten-year-old son, and she's my mother. Couldn't she look into her son's eyes and see what the problem was?

Then I guess it seemed like I wasn't opening up fast enough for her. And Mom's sweet tone quickly turned to one with a little annoyance. She said, "Now, I don't want to play games with you, Alec. What's wrong?"

I got up and walked toward the window. I heard her. I knew she wanted me to answer her, but I needed to talk to God. So, with her watching me, I just got on my knees and started praying silently, *"Lord, I need Your help right now. A part of me wants to call my dad and tell him to get out here right away, but another part of me doesn't want him to be hurt. He's doing such a great job being dad and mom since she's been away. It would hurt me so bad if he lost my mother. So, how do I talk to her? How do I say what I'm feeling? Is it the right thing to do? Help me, please. I don't want to mess up. This is my family. Amen."*

When I got up and turned around, she was standing right in front of me. Her eyes were full of tears.

"Alec, I know this is hard for you because I'm not at home. Every day, I ask myself if I'm doing the right thing."

I wanted to tell her that she is definitely not doing the right thing, but I kept quiet while Mom went on talking.

"I know I'm not perfect, and I make my share of mistakes. I just want you to tell me what's on your mind, Alec. I love you, son."

"And you're not gonna get mad? I can just say whatever I need to, and that's okay?" I asked her, wanting to be sure before I said things that I couldn't take back.

"Come on. Let me fix you some hot chocolate. I know how you like it with tons of marshmallows." She went over to the cabinet and took out a mug, some hot chocolate mix, and a bag of marshmallows.

When I was really little, hot chocolate was one of my favorite drinks. I remember whenever I was a good boy, Mom would come into my room with a cup of hot chocolate. She would sit and watch me drink it, kiss my forehead, and then I'd fall fast asleep.

Well, it wasn't going to calm me down now. Don't get me wrong, I wanted some of that yummy drink. But if she told me that I could say what I needed to say, I was gonna say it.

Five minutes later, she handed me my mug. My eyes got big with excitement, and I couldn't wait to gulp it down. Besides having lots of marshmallows in it, there was loads of whipped cream too. When I put my face to the cup and pulled back, I had a creamy white beard.

She laughed when she saw me, and I didn't want that laugh to leave. But we had to talk about this—for Dad, for Antoine, and for her.

"Now, what's wrong, son?" she asked, as she wiped my face with the napkin she had in her hand.

"Mom, I don't want to go anywhere with Kim. I know he's your friend, and y'all planned a lot of stuff . . . I don't want to spoil any of that . . . but I just want to spend this day with just you and me."

She didn't say anything right away. I was holding my breath, waiting for her to say something. Then I picked up my cup and took another gulp. This time she didn't wipe away the whipped cream on my face. Mom just looked at me with a serious stare until she finally said, "Oh, son."

"Can I ask you a question?" I asked her, trying to figure out the best way to talk about all of this.

"Do you feel the same way about Mr. Kim that you feel about Dad?"

"His name is Mr. Fox, and the answer is no. Why would you ask me that?"

I really didn't care what his name was. It was just good

for me to hear the answer that she gave me. I really wanted to make sure that was how she felt.

So I said, "Are you *sure* you don't like Mr. Fox at all?"

"Alec, where is this coming from?"

"Mom, I think he likes you. Okay?" I finally blurted out.

"He told me so when we were at the Lakers game. And I know Daddy wasn't always that nice to you. So, you have a reason to maybe think about being with somebody else. But Dad is sorry. He loves you, and we have a family. Mr. Fox could mess everything up, and I don't want to be around him."

She patted my back, got up, and walked over to the counter in the kitchen area. I didn't know she had her cell phone until she held it to her ear. A few seconds later, she said, "Hey, this is Lisa. I just wanted you to know that we're not going to go. I want to stay here with Alec. I'll talk to you later. Yeah, have fun with the other cast members. Bye."

Mom walked back over to me and sat down. "I noticed that the past couple of days you haven't been talking much. Ever since that Lakers game I couldn't figure it out, but now I get it. Kim knows that I'm committed to my family. Look, son, I'll deal with him later. For now, it's just me and you. Let's enjoy bringing in the New Year together. Okay?"

She held me and hugged me tight, and right away I started to feel better. Then Mom took a minute and added,

"Alec, don't ever doubt how much I love you and your brother no matter what happens, okay? My little boy is growing up to be quite a little man. Just let me handle this. This is adult stuff. It's hard on you now, but some way or another it will all work out."

Our talk went pretty well, and there was nothing left for me to do but put my faith in God and let Him fix everything. I looked out of the window to see the big blue sky and thanked God for answering my prayer for help.

● ● ●

On the plane ride home, all I wanted to do was get back to Antoine. I wanted to tell him how I kept Mom from spending more time with this dude.

Besides that, I wanted to hear about his basketball tournament. When he picked me up from the airport, Dad told me that Antoine won MVP for the whole competition.

As we walked in the door, instead of feeling happy to be back at home, I was shocked to find that we had company. Aunt Dot and Lil P. were staying with us for the weekend.

I was really annoyed when I found out that not only was Lil P. there, he was staying in my room. After that first night when he shoved me out of my double bed and onto the floor, I slept in the family room on the couch. From then on, I couldn't wait for him to leave.

Antoine and Lil P. had been together a whole day before I got back. And, to me, they were acting a little too tight. Being around them felt like the invasion of the bad boys, and I wasn't gonna let them make me bad too.

Then Dad made us play outside together. I really wasn't happy about that, and Lil P. quickly reminded me why.

"Ouch!" I screamed out, as Lil P. threw the ball at me really hard. Even though I had missed my brother, seeing him and Lil P. laugh at me wasn't cool. I wished I was anywhere but here.

"Quit actin' like a little wimp!" said Lil P., as he knocked my hand off my side. Before I could move away from him, he jabbed me in the chin.

"Look up, man! How you gonna catch the ball if you're lookin' down?"

"I don't wanna play anymore," I quickly shot back.

"Whatever!" Antoine came over, shouting at me. "You're not quittin'!"

Just then, Aunt Dot stood in the doorway and said, "What's all this screamin' I hear goin' on? Y'all gettin' along?"

Before I could tell her the truth and say, *"No, Lil P. is torturing me!"* Antoine pinched me really hard in the side. So, I kept quiet.

Lil P. ran up to her and kissed her on the cheek. "It's all good out here, Grandma."

I waited a minute for Aunt Dot to close the door and said, "You can't tell me that I'm playin' if I don't want to! Move outta my way!"

I was trying my best to get past Antoine. But when I

stepped to the left to go into the house, Lil P. blocked my way. He and Antoine laughed like it was the funniest thing in the world. Then they started shoving me back and forth like I was the basketball.

It was no secret that last summer I had caught up to Antoine in size. But over the last couple of months, he hit a growth spurt and passed me by again. So now, not only was he bigger than me, but Lil P. was bigger than him. The two of them against me was a complete mismatch. It was like our school team playing against a bunch of NBA players.

"Okay, okay, I'll play," I said, figuring I could get them to leave me alone if I just played a little longer.

"And don't try and run away either . . . goin' in the house like a little girl," Lil P. mocked me, as he started dribbling the ball.

Antoine was the ref and I was playing against Lil P. He had five shots and I had two. When I went to dribble the ball and go around him for a layup, he knocked my feet from underneath me. I was in the air and went straight down on my side, hitting the concrete like a ton of bricks.

Antoine rushed over to Lil P. "That's too hard! Not so rough!" he shouted.

But Lil P. pushed him out of the way and shouted at me, "Get on up! Don't act like you're hurt."

It didn't matter what he said because I was hurting and in pain. Something wasn't right about the way the two of them were playing. I didn't care what kind of names they were gonna try and call me, I was done. As soon as I got to my feet, I headed toward the front door.

"You're not goin' anywhere. You're gonna finish the game!" Lil P. yelled at me. As I turned around to tell him that I was done, the basketball hit me square in the nose.

This time when I fell, blood started pouring from my nose like milk from a gallon jug when you try to fill up a glass.

"Ouch! My nose! It's broken!" I yelled out, as I grabbed my face. I was in real pain.

Lil P. teased, "My nose is broken! Na na na na na. Aw, quit whinin'. Your nose ain't broken."

"How do you know?" Antoine asked him. Finally, my brother sounded like he cared about me.

Lil P. grabbed him by the collar. "Chill out! Go in the house and get some paper towels. Wet 'em just a little bit and don't let our grandmas see you! You know how they get."

Antoine did exactly what Lil P. said. I was so mad at my brother, but I couldn't do a thing about it because my nose was bleeding and hurting so bad. I really did think it was broken.

"It hurts! Leave me alone!" I cried out, as I tried to get to the front door.

Lil P. jumped in front of me. He held his fist under my chin so that my head was pushed backward and said, "Hold still! You gotta hold your head up!" Then he whispered in my ear. "If you tell anybody that I did this, your nose really will be broken!"

He wasn't joking, and I knew he wasn't playing. I just

wanted to go inside and get some help, but my attempts didn't work. Lil P. wouldn't let me move. He wasn't going to give me the chance to tell anybody what happened.

When my brother came back outside, both of them pulled me around the side of the house and started acting like doctors. Except, they weren't gentle and their hands weren't clean. The stuff they kept saying to me was awful. I was being bullied by my cousin and my brother. I was just thankful when my nose stopped bleeding.

Lil P. and Antoine stepped away from me and started talking to each other. I could tell they were nervous. They looked at my bloody shirt and I stared hard back at them, waiting to see what they would do next.

A minute or two later, Lil P. came back over to me and said, "You can have your room back. I'm stayin' with Antoine tonight! But you'd better remember what I said. Now, go on in and get cleaned up. Don't let nobody see you. We'll cover for you until dinner."

I couldn't believe this was really happening. Before I started toward the door, I looked at Antoine. He couldn't even look back at me. He couldn't own up to the fact that this was all wrong. With blood covering my shirt, I tried to dash to my room before anyone saw me.

When Grandma came into the hall, I hid from her because I didn't want to get in trouble for not telling. I heard her call out, "Who just ran in here like that?"

Lil P. shielded me so she couldn't see the blood. "It was me, Grandma," I said, as I slid into my room.

Antoine spoke up, "Alec said he has a headache, so I told him to go and get in bed."

Grandma headed toward my door. "Well, let me see about him. He may need some aspirin!"

"He said it's not hurtin' too bad, Auntie Mary," Lil P. said to my grandmother, as he shut my door. "We'll make sure he's okay."

"Aw! Y'all so sweet . . . taking care of my little grand-baby like that. I'm so glad y'all gettin' along."

When she walked away, Lil P. said with pride, "See! We got this." He stood against the door like he was standing guard or something.

"Remember," he said to me. "If you don't want a real broken nose, just forget any of this ever happened."

I really didn't know what to do or say. So, I raced past both of them, dashed in the bathroom, slammed the door, and just cried.

● ● ●

On the first day of class after the holidays, I went back to my old ways. My feelings were hurt because of the bullying I'd been through at home. My nose was still sore, and, since I didn't tell anyone about what had happened, I was really stressed out. I just wanted to be left alone.

I sat alone when our class went to the library. Morgan looked upset too, but I didn't let that bother me. It didn't even matter that Trey couldn't really understand why I was pulling back. They just had to get over it because right now

I had to deal with how I was feeling.

Later on the playground, Trey came over to me and asked, "So, you don't wanna play kickball? Your favorite game." He was trying to get me out of my bad mood. "You can pick the teams," he offered me.

Just then Tyrod ran over and grabbed the ball out of Trey's hands.

"Hey! Give that back to me!" Trey yelled out.

When Trey started chasing after him, Tyrod stopped in front of him and said, "I've got this ball! If you want one, then go over there and get one!"

"But that was the last one, and I had it first," Trey told him.

"Well then, I guess you can't play until I'm done," Tyrod said, as he laughed at my friend.

Knowing Tyrod, when he looked around at the crowd to see who was watching, he was only interested in showing how tough he was. That's when he took his eye off the ball. I quickly walked up to him, grabbed the ball, and handed it back to Trey.

"Leave him alone!" I said to Tyrod, as he tried to take the ball back.

"Aw, forget you guys," Tyrod said, before he ran off to bother some other kid.

"See, I knew you cared!" Trey said to me.

I looked away. Yes, I cared about him. But I still didn't wanna hang out. Why couldn't he get that? He didn't seem to understand that I didn't wanna be pushed right now.

That's when Morgan stepped in and told Trey, "Come on. Some of us are gonna play kickball. Just leave Alec alone."

I wanted to say thank you, but she turned around and jogged away.

I stood there wishing my mom was with me so I could put my head in her lap and have her tell me that everything was gonna be okay. But Mom wasn't here. I had to deal with my own stuff. I had to figure this out for myself.

I thought about trying to talk things over with my brother, but Antoine was nowhere around. Besides, he didn't seem interested in what I was going through. Feeling the way that I was, I might've marched right to my dad's office and talk to him, but I didn't think that was the way to handle this either.

So, I sat down on a swing. And with my hand on my forehead, I just prayed, *"Okay, Lord. I'm back again. I'm tryin' to do everything right. I'm not tryin' to be mean to my friends, but I'm havin' a hard time. The biggest part of my problem is my brother. He's mad at me again. This time it's because I didn't side with him at basketball tryouts. I don't know what to do and I honestly feel that if You don't help me, I'm gonna blow. Who knows what might happen."*

Just then, Trey rushed over to the swing area and told me, "Alec, you've gotta come! You've gotta help!"

"Is Tyrod messin' with you again?" I asked him.

"No, he's not messin' with me . . . you've gotta come and see."

"Well, if he's not messin' with you, then I'm out of it."

"Come on, man, just come!"

Trey finally talked me into it. Not wanting to get involved in anything, I stood up anyway and went over to the crowd.

Tyrod was at it again. He was talking loud and being rude. "I guess Santa Claus didn't come to your house. You still got them old ripped up, tired, ugly, broke down boots," he mocked Gilmer.

Gilmer just gave him a look that said, *Man, are those silly little words supposed to hurt me?* That made Tyrod upset.

"Yeah, we all know you like lookin' like a nerd," Tyrod continued, as the crowd laughed.

Trey urged me, "You've gotta get in there and do something. He won't leave Gilmer alone."

"I'm going to get Mr. Wade," Morgan said in a loud voice.

Trey and I both knew she'd do it because when the two of us were fighting back in the second grade, Morgan was the one who got the teachers to break us up.

"But nobody's fightin'," I said to her.

"Look! Tyrod is about to punch him," said Trey.

Sure enough, Tyrod had stuck his arm out like he was getting ready to sock Gilmer. But, all of sudden, Gilmer caught his fist like he was catching a baseball or something. He twisted Tyrod's hand around so hard that it made him bend down on his knees.

Tyrod squealed real loud, "Ow, ow, ow! That hurts! Let go!"

Gilmer finally let go, and Tyrod started walking backward to get as far away from Gilmer as he could. I knew right then, he didn't need my help. Gilmer had it goin' on.

Watching him in action made me realize what I needed to do. I had to quit being scared and just stand up to people who do wrong—even if that person is my own brother or my cousin. They just needed to be dealt with.

People started calling Tyrod all kinds of mean names. He hated it so much that he got up and ran off. He got what he deserved. Although he tried to hurt Gilmer, he was the one who got hurt instead. Gilmer stopped Tyrod's bullying cold. I was so glad he had taught Tyrod—and me—a good lesson.

Letter to Mom

Dear Mom,

I know I had a sad look on my face when I left Hollywood, but my sadness over being away from you is hard to deal with. Without you, I feel like I have no one to guide me.

I'm sorry for whining in my letters, but after all, I'm just a kid. Not only are you my mom, but you are my hero too. That's why I need you to come home.

Antoine needs you too. He's gone back to bullying me. But I learned from Gilmer, the new boy in my class, that you can't run away from trouble. You have to stand tall and deal with it.

       Your son,
       Trying Not to Fail Alec

Word Search: Basketball Fouls

The game of basketball has rules. You must follow the rules, if you don't want to get your team in trouble. Listed below are some of the most frequent fouls incurred when playing the game of basketball.

```
S  D  N  U  O  B  E  R  C  A  I  E
D  C  O  E  Y  M  S  A  E  Q  L  J
N  K  I  U  R  M  R  Y  T  U  J  T
U  T  S  Y  B  R  D  H  R  A  E  R
O  D  T  R  Y  L  U  C  E  R  R  A
B  S  O  I  E  E  E  E  B  T  S  V
F  I  N  C  Z  S  G  D  Z  E  E  E
O  G  O  A  E  R  P  R  R  R  Y  L
T  P  E  E  O  Q  S  T  A  I  I  I
U  T  R  V  X  O  K  S  L  H  B  N
O  H  L  U  O  F  H  C  E  T  C  G
T  P  R  A  C  T  I  C  I  N  G  S
```

CARRYING   **CHARGE**   **DOUBLEDRIB (Double Dribble)**
OUTOFBOUNDS (Out of Bounds)   **TECHFOUL (Technical Foul)**
THREESECRULE (Three-Second Rule) TRAVELING

BIG trouble

4

"Trey! Come on, man! Let's play my new game on the Xbox," I said to my buddy. He was staying overnight with me because his parents were out of town at a Falcons playoff game.

Having overnight company was new to me. When Trey's parents called, Dad said we would be glad to have him over. Trey and I were having a great time until Antoine saw how happy I was. He had to find a way to spoil our fun.

Antoine was sitting on the couch in the family room, and he called out, "Hey, Trey, you wanna play a racing game on the Wii? It's really cool."

Trey didn't even hesitate to answer. Thinking that Antoine was a cool guy, he was excited to play with my older brother. But Antoine just wanted some attention. He didn't really wanna play with Trey. He just wanted to get back at me.

I know it's true, because the minute he found out that Trey was coming over, Antoine right away said that he didn't want Trey to hang around him. Now, he was trying to steal my buddy's attention away from me.

Later on in the day, when I wanted to watch the Lakers game in the living room with my friend, Antoine said, "Trey, remember that scary movie I was tellin' you about? Well, it's on upstairs. Wanna watch it?"

"Oh, for real? Cool," Trey said, as his eyes got wide with excitement.

Then, just like that, Trey took off! He didn't even say he was going. He didn't even ask if I wanted to watch it with them. He just dashed up the stairs behind Antoine.

Before they took off, Antoine gave me a sly grin, and I just sat there feeling left out.

When it was time for us to go to sleep, I was getting my rollout bed ready so that Trey could crash on it. Before I knew it, Antoine showed up just in time to cause more trouble for me.

He came to my door and said in the most annoying voice, "Trey, man, what you doin' in here? Alec goes to sleep way too early. If you stay in my room, we can tell jokes and ghost stories all night! We'll have a blast!"

There was no time for me to protest. Trey was gone. By now, I was getting used to it and didn't even sweat it. I went down to the kitchen and cut a slice of Grandma's carrot cake. Red velvet was really my favorite, but I could settle for any piece of her delicious cakes anytime. I loved the cream cheese icing on both kinds. Man, that spicy cake tasted so good!

After pouring myself a glass of milk, I sat at the table. With each bite of cake, I was feeling more sorry for myself. My big brother had taken over and was having fun with my company. What was I supposed to do? How could I compete when he was older, funnier, and cooler to be around? Trey didn't even care. He was supposed to hang out with me, but he kept ignoring me like I was a fly on the wall.

Grandma came in and walked over to the sink. It was like she was reading my mind when she said, "Baby, I know you're hurtin'."

"Huh? I mean, ma'am?" I said, thinking she couldn't possibly understand why I was bummed out.

At that moment, I wasn't upset that Mom was away, even though I did long for her to be home. I missed her a lot, but I was proud of her for reaching her dreams. And it wasn't that I was bummed that my grandmother made us keep the house spotless. I found a system to keep my areas clean. It wasn't even about my dad being the assistant principal of my school. I had gotten over that too. So, how could Grandma know how I was feeling?

"I've been watchin' y'all and Antoine is hogging your buddy. I know how it is. My sister used to do the same thing to me," she explained. I sat there listening, surprised that she really did know. "He's tryin' to get up under your skin, but don't let him. If you care about your friend, go up there and talk to him. Let him know how you feel. He should understand."

65

"Yeah, but Trey is acting like he doesn't care how I feel."

"So, make him care. Don't just sit here and act like it's not bothering you. Sometimes friends don't understand when they're doin' a friend wrong. They have to be told. Express yourself. This young man, Trey, has been very respectful all day. He doesn't know what he's doing bothers you."

Then Grandma told me why she knew what I was going through. "One day," she started, "I brought one of my friends over after school, and Dot couldn't have any company. Whenever my parents stepped out the room, Dot was all in Rosie's face. It wasn't until I talked to Rosie that she understood I should have some of her time. She came over to play with me. Either we were gonna do things together, or she was gonna have to go home."

"Grandma, you really told her that?" I asked.

"Child, it's been so long ago I think that's what I said. I do remember when we got to school the next week, Dot didn't want anything to do with Rosie. I tried to tell Rosie. But one day Dot and I worked out our troubles. You and Antoine will do the same. He's your big brother, but that doesn't mean he has to push you around. And he shouldn't be able to take away your friend."

I took my grandmother's advice and went right up to Antoine's room. I couldn't believe he had my friend lying on the floor with no blanket or pillow. Antoine wasn't being kind to Trey at all. They weren't having fun like he promised. Instead, he was asleep and snoring real loud.

I went over to Trey and shook him to see if he was sleeping. He was awake and looked up at me with water in his eyes.

"What's wrong?" I asked him.

"Can I go in your room? Your brother told me that he didn't even want me in here."

"Yeah. Trey, I was a little bummed out that you came over to my house and you were spending most of the time with my brother. That wasn't cool."

"I just thought hanging with someone older was a cool thing to do. Guess not. My bad, man."

We went to my room. And the more we talked it out, I started feeling better. I was glad that we had such a great talk. Now he could understand how I'd been feeling. It finally felt like we could be best friends.

● ● ●

"Where's my hairbrush, Antoine?" I called out.

I was really frustrated with my brother. He had pulled every trick in the book trying to make Trey be his friend. Now he was still trying to mess with me. I couldn't find some of my things, and Grandma told me that she hadn't moved them. Antoine wanted me to think I'd lost my stuff. But I knew where to find my iPod, my Wii controller, my wallet, and my watch. All the fingers pointed to Antoine.

Now my hairbrush was missing too. I knew exactly where I put it, and Antoine wasn't gonna get away with saying he hadn't moved it.

I walked to his room and demanded, "So where is it?"

"Where's what?"

"My hairbrush. You heard me callin' you."

"Why would I wanna have that?"

"I'm not sayin' you used it, but I know you moved it. Now, where is it?"

"I told you, I don't have it."

I didn't waste another minute, I just left out of his room, yelling, "Dad!"

Antoine quickly brushed by me and dashed into the bathroom.

"Look, it was sitting right here on the counter the whole time."

I went to look again. "It wasn't there a minute ago. I'm not that blind. You just put it back and you know it."

When Dad came into the bathroom to see what was going on, Antoine tried to sound pitiful. "He keeps accusing me of stuff, Dad. I told him I didn't do it."

"Dad, he keeps movin' stuff. He just wants to bug me," I argued.

"You guys need to do something constructive," Dad cut in and said. "Antoine, I got an e-mail from your teacher about your upcoming math test. Alec helped you before, and maybe he can help you again."

I just looked at Dad and said nothing. Was he serious?

Antoine smiled, knowing he wasn't in trouble for taking my things. And, on top of that, now I'd have to do something for him.

"You got a problem with that?" Dad asked, when I didn't reply.

Actually, I did have a problem with it. I didn't like how my brother was treating me, and I didn't want to help him. I knew Dad could make me. But if he knew how my brother was treating me, maybe he would back off of me and put more attention on Antoine.

"He doesn't want me to help him, Dad," I said, looking at Antoine.

"Oh, yeah! I wanna get help from Alec, Dad. I know that if he helps me, then I'll be a genius," Antoine said, in a teasing voice. He gave me a wink and handed me my hair brush. "Here you go, little brother. See, I helped you find something. Now you can help me."

All of a sudden, the ball was back in my court. But I wasn't gonna serve it up the way Antoine wanted. So, I said, "Okay. I don't want to help him, Dad. That's it. He's not tellin' the truth, and I'm not helpin' him."

The way I stormed out of that bathroom and slammed my room door meant instant trouble. I stood close by the door, just knowing that Dad was gonna come in any minute and punish me.

Just as I knew he would, Dad opened up my door. "Alec, you're going to do what I tell you to do. I know it's hard right now, not having our whole family together, but I will not allow outbursts like you just did. You're going to have to talk to me, son. I thought you and Antoine were past all your problems. Now, what's going on with you?"

Finally, this was my moment to share with my dad. But I hoped he was ready to hear all I had to say because I wasn't gonna hold back.

"What's on your mind, son?"

After a couple of minutes passed, I hadn't said anything. So Dad assured me, "Don't worry, this is just between the two of us."

I said, "Give me a second, Dad." I felt the need to say a prayer before I opened up to him. Dad nodded like he understood, and I prayed, *"God, please help me. I want to talk to my dad about so many things. I need to share my feelings with him about Mom, Antoine, and the crazy things going on at school. But, I don't wanna make things worse. Please give me the right words to say. Amen."*

After I was done with my prayer, I sighed. My dad looked at me and said, "Do you want us to pray together?"

He shocked me because so far we only held hands and prayed at dinnertime. We never prayed together like this before.

Dad didn't even give me a chance to answer. He started praying, *"Father, I come to You right now, thankful for my son, Alec. I know that at his age things can be tough. It can't be easy not to have his mom around or having a brother who gives him a hard time. Please help him to trust You and to know that I care. He needs to know that I'm here for him. In Jesus' name. Amen."*

Suddenly, I felt a sigh of relief and everything just came pouring out. "Dad, first of all, that boy, Tyrod, is so mean. He picks on everybody. I try to help, but I don't know how."

Dad stopped me right there and said, "Let's not focus on anyone else. As long as you're doing what's right, things will work out in the end. What else?"

"Antoine. He keeps bullying me. I don't want you to get mad at him or say anything to him. It'll just make things worse. No matter what I say, he's always upset with me."

"Why do you think he's always upset with you?"

I didn't wanna get Antoine in trouble by telling all the wrong things he's done, like hitting Jelani for no reason. Somehow, Antoine talked his way out of trouble when the coach addressed that with my father. Dad and Coach gave Antoine a warning not to cause any trouble. He had one more chance to play right or he was going to get kicked off the team.

So instead, I talked about football. "We've never really been on the same page since he felt like I took his spot on the football team. But, Dad, I didn't make the coach pick me to start. Please don't say anything to him about this. He'll just deny that it's a problem."

"Understood," he said, as he placed his hand on my shoulder. "Now, how do you feel about your mom?"

"I miss her and love her so much. Dad, I think you should go and see her. She said she loves you and misses us, but I think the two of you need to talk. All of this stuff keeping the two of you apart is bothering me. Can you fix it? Will you fix it?"

"I'll try my best to make things right, and I'll watch things at school more closely. Don't worry, Alec, things will get better. Don't forget that we prayed. Now, you can relax and know that God is with us. And, remember, you can always talk to me, son."

My chest felt so much better after I let all my worries out. And my dad had listened. Whew!

● ● ●

"Thank you for giving me a Valentine's card and candy," Morgan said, as she sat next to me in the schoolyard.

"It's no big deal. You're my friend."

"But you didn't give any to the whole class."

Truth was, I'd been feeling kinda bad about not being a good friend to Morgan. When I went to the drugstore with Dad the other day, he said that I could buy the $3 box of chocolates. Still, I wouldn't have done anything if I knew she was going to make a big deal about it. I thought to myself, *Just eat it. Enjoy it. Man, quit talkin' about it already!*

Then Morgan reached over and gave me a hug. "Thanks again, Alec. Now all of the girls in our class think I'm really cool because I got some candy from a boy."

I looked away and didn't say anything. It was good that I made her happy, but again it was no big deal.

When I tried to get up and walk away, Morgan said, "Are you okay? Are the other boys picking on you or something?"

"I don't care about that. Really."

"Yeah? So then, what's goin' on with you?"

Morgan never backed down from an issue. I kinda liked that about her. If she cared about you, she really let you know it. That was cool.

Then all of a sudden, we heard a lot of noise. When we looked up, we saw Trey jumping up and down like he was trying to get our attention.

"What's goin' on with him?" Morgan asked.

All of the fourth grade classes were out on the playground at one time. Leave it up to Trey to be in the middle of everything. He saw us looking at him and waved his hands for us to join him.

When we didn't go to him, he came over to us. "Didn't y'all see me callin' you?" asked Trey.

"We're talking."

"Okay, forget it," Trey said, a little annoyed. Then he left us and ran over to our buddy from last year, Billy.

Morgan and I continued our talk. "So, tell me what's goin' on? Is it your mom?"

"Things could be better, but you know she came to visit for Thanksgiving. And then I went to visit her for Christmas. My dad went out there to see her over the weekend. He took her a Valentine's Day gift."

"That's good, right? Everything is working out?"

"I guess."

73

"Don't worry about anything, Alec. You know, God can work things out for your good."

"Morgan, what does that really mean?" I asked.

"It means what it says. Pray about it, give it to God, and let Him fix the problem. When God works something out, whatever happens, you can live with it. It'll be okay because He knows best."

"Is it okay that your parents aren't together anymore?" I asked her.

"It wasn't at first. It really hurt back then. Now I'm older and I can deal with it better. When I think about it, in the beginning, I couldn't handle my mom being married to someone else. But it's best. Daddy Derek makes her smile and tells her she's pretty. She loves that. She's so happy, and that's all that matters."

I said, "Well, my mom is already supposed to love three men. There's no room for anyone else."

"Alec, if that's the way it's supposed to be, then don't worry about it. Have faith and let God handle it."

I started thinking about everything Morgan told me. She is so wise, and I know she cares. She gives good advice whether I want to hear it or not.

Our talk ended there because Trey came back over to us. Now a big crowd was gathering. The way they were screaming and shouting, I could tell Tyrod had something to do with it.

Morgan said, "Trey, what's up over there?"

"It's Tyrod. He's pickin' on Gilmer again."

"Gilmer already proved he can handle Tyrod," I said.

"Yeah. Gilmer can handle Tyrod, but he can't handle Tyrod and five other boys. We gotta help my home boy."

"He's not your home boy. He hasn't played with you yet," Morgan said. "It's been, what? Two months?"

"Not even two months," I said in a joking way.

Trey shook his head like he was really worried. The way he did that made me think about it. Trey was right. Gilmer couldn't handle those other boys. I knew he wasn't my friend, but it wouldn't be right to watch him get jumped on. I'd want someone to step in to help me if I was outnumbered. So I stood up. Then Trey and I ran over to where the crowd was to give Gilmer some help.

Tyrod was saying to him, "So, you think you're all that? You think you can just push me around and have people laugh at me? Well, I got friends. Look around, country boy. I got friends!"

"Yeah, I heard you messed with my boy," one boy spoke up and said. He was twice the size of Tyrod.

Another boy tall enough to be in the NBA said, "That's my boy. We were in different rooms, but we hung out all last year. If you mess with him, you mess with us."

Two other guys just stood by looking mean. Another one looked scared and acted like he didn't wanna join in. But, he would make it six against one.

"All right, y'all. Let's get 'em. Let's take 'em down."

They all circled around Gilmer. Tyrod's crew took one step closer. A big group of kids were pushing each other because everyone wanted a front-row view. I looked around to find help. Someone needed to step in, because at that moment, there was no order on the playground. For all of us, there was about to be big trouble.

Letter to Mom

Dear Mom,

I have a lot to tell you, so let me get right to it. I thought it was necessary to tell Dad that he needed to see you. Mom, I really hope that the two of you worked things out while he was there.

Lately, my relationship with Antoine has really been hard. Grandma said she and her sister didn't used to get along but, as they grew older, they got over their issues. She told me that Antoine and I would grow out of it too. I really hope so.

Dad said we need to do more constructive things with our time. The problem with that is he wants me to help Antoine with his math again because I'm pretty good at it. Antoine wants the help, and I feel outnumbered. But, Mom, I shouldn't have to help someone that is mean to me.

Your son,
Trying to Get Order Alec

Word Search: NBA Teams

Many young men dream of being an NBA player. That's because being in the National Basketball Association is the highest level one can play on in the game of basketball. Below are some of the top teams in the NBA.

```
S T A F F I U K C N L C
D L S Y Y Z N T W R A H
A N L O T I D A D Y M E
N G D U C Z A E H Z E E
M X O K B L U H Z P L R
G S S G C M U A U I S I
U X Y Z I E J T B W L N
M T H N J U L D N K A G
S K W A H U S T R X K K
W L J R O U N D I Q E W
K M W V N P D Q L C R O
F A S T P A C E D J S D
```

BULLS   CELTICS   HAWKS   HEAT   JAZZ   KNICKS   LAKERS

BROKEN UP

5

"Alec, you've got to do something! You have to get in there! Help Gilmer out, man," Trey said to me, as we stood back and watched the arguing.

"No! Don't you go in there, something could happen to you if you try to help! I'm serious, Alec! It's five of them against one," Morgan said, holding my arm to keep me back.

One friend was telling me to get involved, and the other one was telling me to stay out of it. I didn't know what I wanted to do. This was way too much drama. Besides, it wasn't my problem. Tyrod and his friends weren't ganging up on me. I wasn't in the middle of the circle with all those unfriendly people shoving and talking mean to me.

But then again, I thought about the fact that I had accepted Christ in my heart. Because of that, I knew that I should always ask, *"What Would Jesus Do?"* I don't think He'd just stand on the sidelines and let somebody get hurt.

It wasn't fair and it wasn't right. Wasn't it my duty to do something?

Tyrod was staring Gilmer down and stepped in tighter so Gilmer couldn't move. "Uh huh, you think you're so big and bad . . . comin' up to me and tryin' to embarrass me in front of everybody! What you gonna do now?"

Tyrod shoved Gilmer hard. At first, Gilmer didn't move. Tyrod huffed and puffed and shoved him again. This time he pushed Gilmer into his really tall friend, whose name is Zarick.

Zarick said, "Yeah. You walk around here thinkin' you're better than all of us."

"What are you talkin' about?" Gilmer finally opened up his mouth to speak. "You're makin' up stuff. I don't think I'm better than nobody. Move and let me pass!"

Zarick didn't move. All five of the boys took another step toward Gilmer to keep him from moving.

"They're gonna beat him up in a minute, man. We've gotta do something. If you don't wanna do it, then I'm goin' in there to fight," said Trey.

Morgan looked at him and said, "What can you do by yourself?"

Trey said with boldness, "I'm not gonna stand here and be a chicken. It can't be five against one. Even if Gilmer is the toughest thing since the Karate Kid, he can't fight all those dudes. So I'll do it if Alec won't."

Morgan said, "Please, the Karate Kid took on a bunch of boys all at once?"

80

"No, it wasn't the Karate Kid, it was his teacher," Trey argued back.

I just let the two of them go back and forth about that. The fight in front us had my attention. Deep down, I didn't want anyone to get hit or hurt, especially Trey.

But Trey had a big heart. He proved to me a couple of years ago that he was tough on the inside. Trey stood up to me when I bullied him. Besides, he hadn't grown as much as some of us over the two years. So Trey needed to stay back. The boys circling Gilmer were huge.

Without thinking too hard about it, I reached out and caught Tyrod's arm when he lifted it. "Now, you're gonna have to hit me too."

"What? Right now, I don't have a problem with you, London. You need to step to the side." Then Tyrod thought for a second and said, "Come over here and let me talk to you for a second."

When we stepped away from the crowd, Tyrod said, "Why do you wanna get into this, man?"

"What you're doin' isn't right."

"And you comin' all up in the middle is right?"

"Yeah, I had to do something. No kind of fighting is good. But, if you're gonna fight, it should be one on one— you and Gilmer. But you don't wanna do it that way. You've got all your boys goin' up against one person. I'm not gonna let that happen. That's not cool. That's not right. And that's not fair."

"What's up over there, Tyrod?" Zarick called to him.

"He wants some of this action too!" Tyrod said, pointing at me.

If it's got to be like that, it's okay with me. I didn't care if I was at school at that point. I didn't care that I might get hurt. I didn't care that my dad could walk up at any minute and I'd be in big trouble. Gilmer was outnumbered, and Trey had a point. Somebody needed to do something.

Then Trey yelled out, "We're goin' to get his dad!"

Zarick said, "His dad? Who they talkin' about?"

"You know, his dad is the assistant principal."

"Man, I ain't tryin' to mess with him then," replied Zarick.

Tyrod went over to Zarick, grabbed his collar, and said, "You ain't gonna leave right now. We're in the middle of this, and we're gonna finish it. We can handle this before his dad even comes. They can't do nothin' to all of us. Let's take care of these two wimps."

"Why are you all standin' around here waitin' for a fight?" Morgan screamed out to the crowd.

Tyrod answered her, "They're ready to see somebody get their nose bashed in."

I'd had it with Tyrod's junk, so I said, "I'm standin' right here, Tyrod. I haven't seen you raise your hand and swing at me like you did Gilmer."

"Oh, so you're gonna take me on?"

"That's it. I'm leavin'," said Zarick.

Tyrod told him again, "You ain't goin' anywhere."

Zarick shot back, "Don't tell me what I'm not gonna do!"

"I said you're not goin'!" Tyrod responded in a stronger tone.

All of a sudden, Trey came rushing back. But he wasn't alone.

"Oooh, it's Dr. London," some kids started yelling out, as they backed away.

Then it dawned on me. I did care that I was about to get in trouble. Would my dad understand why I stood up? Why I got involved? Or, why I couldn't let everything go down like this?

"Boys, back away from each other! Kids, every one of you get back to class now! Recess is over. Everybody go inside!" my dad said with a powerful voice.

All we needed was an adult to take charge, because as soon as he said it, everybody scattered.

When Tyrod and his buddies tried to get away, my dad said, "No, young men, you five stand right over here." He pointed at Gilmer and then he pointed at me. "You two, stand here."

When he asked what had happened, everyone was quiet.

I looked up at the sky. My dad looked at me and gave me a very hard stare.

I prayed. *"Lord, I tried to do the right thing. I try to help other people, but I keep gettin' myself into more and more trouble. I think I'm doin' what You want me to do, but, by the way my dad is looking at me . . . I'm in trouble again. Can't You help me like I tried to help Gilmer? I would really appreciate it, even though he doesn't look like he appreciated it. I don't know, Lord, this just isn't right."*

"Oh, you all don't want to talk. No one wants to tell me what happened. Then, you know what, everybody go to my office! All seven of you, right now!" Dad's command was in a stronger voice than I'd heard him use in a long time.

I knew this wasn't gonna be good. On the way to my dad's office, I was walking close to Tyrod. I didn't want to walk near my dad. He was in the back of us with Gilmer. We all knew where his office was, so we didn't need him to lead the way.

But why was I surprised to hear Tyrod talk junk to his crew? "Look," he said. "All we gotta do is just be quiet. We gotta stick together. Nobody say a word. Dr. London can't break us down. I told you guys all of us can't get in trouble. If all of us stick to the same story, then those two wimps can't touch us. All right? Come on. Zarick, man, wassup?"

Zarick looked over at me with a frown on his face. Then he looked back at Tyrod and said, "All right, I'm with you, man. Nothin' happened, and I dare anybody to say anything different."

Tyrod started laughing as he got closer to me and whispered, "And if your dad tries to get me in trouble, my mama is gonna come up here. I already told her that our assistant principal doesn't like his son because I'm in his class!"

"Huh?" I said, knowing that what he said didn't really

make sense. "You told your mom that my dad—"

Tyrod cut me off. "Ugh! Don't try and get under my skin. What I said made sense. Got it?"

Zarick said, "It really didn't, T."

"Quiet!" my dad called out. "Everyone walk in silence."

From then on, I kept my mouth shut. I was happy Zarick told Tyrod what he said didn't make sense. Maybe in my dad's office Zarick would stand up and tell the truth again. Tyrod always thought he knew everything. I was pretty sure he was trying to say that my dad favored me because I was his son. But that's not what he said.

A few minutes later, all seven of us were in my dad's office. My father looked at me and said, "All right, Alec, talk to me. What exactly happened?"

"How you gonna ask your son?" Tyrod interrupted.

"Young man, I'm going to give you a chance to speak. However, right now is not the time. I'll let you know when it's your turn to speak. Alec, talk to me and don't be afraid to tell me what happened."

"I'm not scared, Dad," I said with a slight attitude.

"Watch yourself and get rid of the attitude," my father quickly scolded me.

"Yes, sir," I added. Then I explained what happened on the playground. "Tyrod and his friends were ganging up on Gilmer. I didn't think it was right, so I stepped in. I didn't hit anybody, but—"

"I didn't hit nobody either!" Tyrod yelled out before I finished talking.

"Tyrod, this is your last warning," my dad told him.

"That's pretty much what happened, Dad."

Tyrod raised his hand and bounced up and down like it was an emergency and he had to say something right away. "Can I talk now? Can I please talk? Are you gonna believe me, or are you just gonna believe your son?"

My dad said, "Young man, you're very close to getting an in-school suspension. And that's before I find out if you were in the wrong here."

"But I didn't do nothin', Dr. London," Tyrod said, calming down a bit.

"You're being disrespectful in my office. I've told you to settle down and I'll give you a chance to speak, but you just keep talking out of turn."

"Okay, well, I'm sorry. Can I talk now? Can I say something?"

"Yes, you may. Tell me your side of the story."

"Thank you, sir," Tyrod said, trying to get in good with my father. "You know, we were just playin' on the playground . . . just shootin' some hoops . . . and this dude . . ."

He pointed toward Gilmer. Then Gilmer spoke up and said, "I have a name."

"This guy, this, this, Gilmer guy," Tyrod said, as if saying the boy's name was going to cause him pain. "He got in our way. We weren't tryin' to mess with him. Right, you guys? Ask Zarick, Dr. London . . . Z, tell him."

"Young man, talk to me," Dad said, looking at Zarick. "Is that what happened?"

Zarick held his head down. "Uh, yeah. Yes, sir. Yep, that's what happened."

My dad turned to Gilmer. "Gilmer, you talk to me. What happened?"

After a long pause, Gilmer said, "It was no big deal."

"That's all you're going to tell me? It's no big deal?" Dad asked him.

I couldn't believe this. I wanted to stand up, throw my hands in the air, stomp my feet, and hit the desk. This was just crazy. Dad had to know that Gilmer was holding something back. Tyrod and Zarick were about to get away with telling a big fib, but I had to be cool. I just sat there, gritting my teeth and shaking my head.

"Okay, since we have such opposite sides of the story, it looks like no punches were thrown. At least, we can all agree on that. Therefore, I'm going to give all of you warnings this time. If you come back into my office this year for any reason, I won't be as nice."

Hearing my dad say that was just like hearing him say he didn't trust me. He knew I wouldn't lie to him. Not about something as serious as this. I told the truth. I helped someone and tried to make sure that no one got hurt. I got in the middle of it to protect Gilmer, and Dad was saying he really didn't know what happened because there were two different versions of the story. Dad knew Tyrod wasn't honest. Tyrod and I had been in his office before because of his cheating and trying to get me into trouble.

Now, why is Dad acting like he couldn't figure this out

when I told him exactly what was going on? This was so frustrating.

"In addition to this warning, I want you young men to listen to me. You are all in school to learn. It's okay to make friends, but it's not okay to let people lead you down the wrong path," my dad said, looking right at Zarick.

"I can't make nobody do nothin'," Tyrod said under his breath.

"And, son, I'm not saying that you can. But, let me be clear, if I see any of you in my office again you are going to receive the appropriate discipline. This is your final warning. In addition, it is too bad that you all are missing good instruction right now by being in my office and not in class."

He looked around at all seven of us, and went on. "You don't have to take problems upon yourself to fix. Go to a teacher or to any school official. That's why we're here. We expect you to learn. All of you young men have great potential."

"I know I do," Tyrod said, sticking out his chest.

"Then act like it!" Dad patted him on the back and told him. "Now everyone get on out of here and go to class! The secretary will give you passes."

I turned around to say something to my dad and he pointed toward the door for me to exit his office too. Whoever thought he gave me special treatment because I was his son was wrong.

All the rest of the guys went on to class, but Tyrod

BROKEN UP

stood outside my dad's office and waited for me. With his arms folded, he looked at me like, *"Uh huh, you thought I was gonna get in trouble. Huh?"*

"I don't have anything to say to you," I said, as I walked by him.

He caught up with me and told me, "I've got somethin' to say to you, and you're gonna listen. You ever get in my business again, you're gonna really wish you hadn't!"

"Don't threaten me."

"I'm just sayin' mind your own business or you're gonna be sorry. 'Cus the bones I was gonna break on somebody else is gon' be somebody else's."

"Huh?" I said to him, letting him know that what he said made no sense.

"I mean . . . you know what I mean!"

"No, I don't know what you mean, and I don't care. You stay away from me. And, don't worry, I'm gonna stay away from you."

Heading to our classroom, I speeded up because I didn't want to walk with him.

● ● ●

"What are you back there grumbling about, Alec?" My dad said to me, as we were on our way back to school for an evening basketball game.

Sitting in the backseat of the car, I was thinking out loud, but I didn't realize that my mouth was moving too. Causing drama with my father was not something I wanted

89

to do. It's just that I was still upset with everything that happened earlier in the day.

Antoine spoke up, "He's just jealous that I'm still in the starting lineup!"

I didn't know why he didn't get it through his thick skull that we were on the same team. I wanted to win. He was a better basketball player than me. The team we were going up against was undefeated. We needed him to play, and I had no problem with that.

Through the rearview mirror, Dad saw me shaking my head.

"Okay, if it's not that, Alec, talk to me. What is it? Are you upset about what happened at school?"

I looked down, and then I looked out the window. I didn't want to answer him because I didn't want any more trouble. But maybe by not answering it, I was telling him all he needed to know. Besides, I was super hot that he didn't take my side.

"Oh, what happened at school today?" Antoine jumped in and asked.

Antoine really could get under my skin. He always wanted something to be wrong with me. He was happy that my life wasn't perfect. He was such a mean brother.

Dad said, "Not a big deal. He was just in my office today."

"Ooohhh, you were in Dad's office!" he said, looking at me with a big grin. "Tell me, Dad, what's up? What happened?" he asked our father.

"I said no big deal, son."

"Naw, Dad. Just tell him. You believed all the other kids over me anyway. Just tell him."

"Son, that's not what happened."

"Yes it is, Dad. You want me to be honest. You want me to speak my mind. You told me not to be a pushover. But when I say what's on my heart, I'm being disrespectful. I don't know what you want from me! It just doesn't make any sense."

"Daddy, you gonna let him talk to you like that?" Antoine said, trying to get Dad angry with me.

"Antoine, sit over there and hush up. In a few minutes, you're going to have your hands full with the other team."

"Please, I can handle them," he bragged.

Dad warned him, "Boy, don't get too full of yourself!"

"I got skills, Dad. That's just confidence."

"People who have a big head usually don't do so well," Dad said coolly.

He got Antoine then. My brother just put his head back and closed his eyes like he didn't want to hear any more. Then Dad turned his attention back to me.

"Alec, while you might think what happened earlier today was a result of what you said, you're absolutely wrong. In my heart, I strongly believe you were telling the honest truth. That kid in your class was being ganged up on, and you stepped in. I know that."

"So, why didn't you do something then?" I asked in a respectful voice. I really wanted to know.

"Because, what I believe in my heart and what I can prove with facts are two completely different things. You even told me the other day that one of your big problems is that people feel like you get special attention because you're my son. Yet I treat you like I treat everybody else. If the guy for whom you came to the rescue would have stepped up and admitted the fact that it went down exactly like you said it did, then there would've been a different outcome. I won't put up with any bullying on my watch. But, for some reason, he didn't back up your story."

I listened to Dad, but I still wasn't sure that he did the right thing.

"While you might have thought my actions weren't fair, they were just," Dad continued.

I let out a long sigh. "So, Tyrod just keeps gettin' away with stuff."

We pulled up to the gym and Dad parked. Before he hopped out of the car, Antoine asked, "You want me to come to your school and take care of him?"

"Nobody is going to be taking care of nobody," Dad said. "Go on in, boy. We'll be there in just a second. You can tell Coach I'm talking to Alec."

Still angry, I said, "I don't need him to take care of Tyrod for me. I can do it myself."

"That's the wrong talk, son. Like I told all of you guys . . . you come in my office again and it's not going to be good. First I'm going to wear the assistant principal hat and after that I'll wear the dad hat too."

From the look on my face he could tell I wasn't clear. So he explained, "That means I will discipline you in school, and then I'll deal with you again when you get home. No fighting at school!"

"But, Dad, you're just makin' it all worse. He's threatening me and everything."

"Why didn't you tell me that he threatened you?"

"You told me to go to class when I tried talking to you. And the stuff I did tell you, you didn't do anything about. I don't know what to do. I thought I was doing right, trying to help somebody else, and all it did was mess up stuff between me and you. If Tyrod and his friends would've hurt Gilmer, I could hear my dad, not the assistant principal, asking me why I didn't do something. You didn't teach me to be a wimp. You told me to stand up for people who need help standing up for themselves."

"I know, son. I did, and now I have to take back some of my own words. Being the assistant principal of your school is difficult. Trust me, I understand what you're going through. There are kids who don't know how to get along with others. I don't know why, but they don't. I have to be patient with them because some kids do have a lot going on in their lives."

"Tyrod said that his mom would blame the school if he got in trouble."

"That's not correct. I've spoken with his mom and we're on the same page. But, don't you worry about any of that. We just need to pray for their family. You know, tough times can make a person act out. We need to give Tyrod some grace."

What my dad said made a lot of sense, but I still didn't like it. It felt just like taking medicine. It's good for you, but doesn't taste good going down.

When we got inside the gym, the game had already started. Antoine had the ball, but I was surprised when he got a mean jab to his chin from another player.

"Dad, did you see that?"

"No, what? I missed it."

"That guy just hit Antoine in the face!"

Antoine was tough and shook it off. Then, a few plays later, he got pushed real hard by another player on the other team.

"They're not playin' fair," I said.

"I know. I don't like this," Dad said, as he got up and walked toward the bench.

I could see the frustration on Antoine's face. He didn't like it either. A part of me was thinking, *Oh well, now he's getting to see what it's like to have somebody pushing him around.* He and Lil P. had done pretty much the same thing to me.

Before Dad could tell the coach to stop those boys from playing so rough, one of them gave Antoine a really hard punch. Antoine dropped the ball, and the other guy took my brother's arm and twisted it hard behind his back. Antoine fell to the floor and started yelling. I had a feeling that his arm wasn't just messed up, it was broken up.

Letter to Mom

Dear Mom,

There was a lot of trouble at school today. Tyrod and his friends surrounded Gilmer during recess. I jumped in to help him, and Dad took us all to the office.

Tyrod thought Dad was gonna side with me. But when Dad talked to us, he gave us all the same warning. He let us know that he wasn't going to play favorites.

Then Dad told me, as the administrator, he needed more proof than just one person's word against all the other boys. Yep, even Gilmer didn't speak up. I couldn't believe that the boy I was trying to help said nothing. I was mad about that, but Dad explained that he needed at least one of them to back up my story.

Mom, I miss you. Oh, by the way, Antoine got hurt during the game. I'm sure Dad will tell you all about that.

Your son,
Trying to Stay Together Alec

Word Search: Division I Teams

In the spring, March Madness captures the hearts of Americans. Listed below are some of the schools that are usually in the big tournament.

```
B  C  D  T  E  C  H  G  S  Y  S  E
T  D  O  U  J  X  G  E  E  K  J  S
S  W  T  N  K  O  O  O  D  C  T  U
I  T  L  A  N  E  D  R  H  U  W  C
G  E  C  H  N  E  O  G  K  T  Z  A
N  C  O  N  W  I  C  E  F  N  V  R
A  C  U  Z  T  B  L  T  I  E  C  Y
L  Q  R  F  N  Y  X  O  I  K  P  S
S  F  T  C  P  A  L  W  R  C  T  Z
D  R  U  B  T  S  J  N  O  A  U  P
T  S  N  A  G  I  H  C  I  M  C  T
P  Y  L  A  C  U  T  I  P  S  I  N
```

CONNECTICUT   DUKE   GEORGETOWN   KENTUCKY
MICHIGANST (Michigan State)   NCAROLINA (North Carolina)
SYRACUSE

STAND tall

6

"**Dad, Antoine and** I wanna walk to the mini-mart." I thought it was better to be honest with Dad, hoping that he would let us venture out and explore a bit.

He shook his head no. "That's not a good idea for you and Antoine to do. His arm was broken just two days ago. He needs to take it easy. No walking to the store."

I looked over at Antoine. He looked funny trying to eat cereal with his left hand. Antoine looked up and rolled his eyes at me, as though he didn't want me to ask Dad for permission. But I just thought that if we asked first it would keep us from getting in trouble. Antoine probably figured Dad would say no, and we should just go without asking. That way we wouldn't get in trouble because Dad never said we couldn't go.

Now that Dad said no, I guess I blew Antoine's plan. There's no way we should go without Dad's permission.

Still, I am a London. I am my father's son and can't

give up that easy. Dad taught me to be strong and to fight for what I wanted.

"But, Dad!"

"Don't 'but Dad' me, Alec. And don't try to change my mind. It's too dangerous. The store is too far away. Besides, I'll be gone most of the day. You know I have to take Grandma to the doctor. Just relax. I know it's the weekend and you need something to do. How about spending some time studying for the CRCT? I'm sure you remember taking the standard test last year. Well, it's coming up again. If you guys really want to do something positive together, then stay inside and hit the books."

Antoine put down his spoon and said, "But, Dad, this time around it doesn't matter if we pass the CRCT. I took it in the fifth grade and Alec took it in the third. You know too much stress for kids isn't good."

"Boy, don't give me that. Don't ever get too comfortable with your grades. You should always want to excel in school beyond what's in front of you. Just because you don't have to pass by the state's standards doesn't mean you don't have to pass by mine. And you need extra studying."

"Dad, why do I need extra studying?"

"Because of what I just said."

"Well, I just got a B."

"Antoine, please, just chill out today. Rest your arm. Besides studying, you can play your Xbox with one hand. Grandma already made your lunch. It's in the refrigerator. Take it easy."

"Hey, boys!" Grandma greeted us, as she walked into the kitchen. "I made y'all some spaghetti and meatballs. That should hold you until we get back. I'm ready, Andre. For goodness sake, I don't need to go to no doctor. I feel fine."

"I know you don't want to go, Mom," Dad said to her. "But, to make you better, sometimes you have to do what you don't want to do. So, let's go."

"I'm goin'," she moaned, as she left the kitchen. Then she picked up her purse and slowly walked to the door.

As soon as they were gone, Antoine looked at me like he was ready to punch me in my arm or something. Then he reached for his cereal bowl like he was mad enough to pick it up and pour milk all over my head.

"Don't even think about it!" I yelled out, backing away from the table. "It's better for us to know we can't go than to go and get caught. Who wants to be in trouble?"

"I told you not to say nothin'. You didn't wanna go with me because you're a little chicken. Bawk, bawk, bawk, bawk. That's fine, but you're not gonna mess up my chance. I'm goin' to the store anyway. If Dad calls, you better not—and I mean—better not—tell him that I'm gone."

Antoine went over to the sink, washed out his bowl, and put it on the counter. Then he headed up to his room to get dressed. In a flash, he was ready to walk out the door. I was already dressed too. Even though Dad told us no, the curious part of me still wanted to go.

"Uh oh, rebel. I see ya. Dad said no, but you're still down for the ride. You might be a cool little bro after all. C'mon, give me some dap," he said, holding out his cast to me.

We laughed. Then I sighed, as I tried to find the nerve to venture out. A few seconds later, we were headed out the door.

"How much money you got?" Antoine asked me.

I didn't bother to answer him. In the back of my mind, I was still asking myself was this really a good idea. We kept walking, but the store was so far away that I couldn't even see it yet. As soon as we got to the main street, there were tons of cars driving super fast across the big street. The store was on the other side, so sooner or later we were going to have to cross it.

"Maybe this wasn't such a good idea. I'm going back," I said, turning around.

"We're almost there now. Just pick up the pace," Antoine said, grabbing my sleeve so I wouldn't back out.

I wanted to hurry, so I walked a little faster. I wanted to run so bad. We passed by a house that had two junk cars in the front yard. One of the windows was missing a shutter. There was a sign on the broken fence that read "Beware of the Dogs." Before I could even open my mouth, we heard barking.

Antoine shouted for me to watch out. I looked behind and there were three pit bulls gaining on us. Though we were both athletic, there was no way we could move fast enough to get away from those vicious dogs. I just knew those mean, growling dogs were gonna catch us.

"Come on, climb this tree!" Antoine shouted. He wasn't about to let having only one good arm stop him from getting to safety.

The way I was having trouble grabbing the limbs, it seemed like I was the one with my arm in a sling. Just as I tried again to jump up and catch a branch, one of the dogs snagged my pant leg. That gave me the worst feeling in my stomach. It felt like I had eaten too much turkey and dressing and was ready to bust wide open.

"Hurry up! Climb! Come on! Jump up, Alec!" yelled Antoine.

I tried with all my might to get up the tree. I didn't wanna get bit. No way. It seemed like it took me forever, but I made it.

As soon as we were high enough to escape the dogs, Antoine pulled out his cell phone to call Dad.

Sitting up in that tree, it felt like we waited a million years. Even though we knew we were in big trouble, when Dad and Grandma finally made it to us, we were so glad to see them.

Dad went and got the owner of the dogs. The man apologized that they had gotten loose. I was happier than if I'd made my first slam dunk when he put those dogs on leashes and took them far away from us. Finally, it was safe for us to climb back down.

Needless to say, Dad wasn't thrilled with us. On the car

ride home, he didn't say anything to us. It was Grandma whose words made us feel so bad.

She broke the silence and said, "Boys, your daddy does everything he can to keep y'all safe. He asks you to do one thing and you just up and disobey him. He's so hurt right now. I can't believe you two did what you wanted to anyway. I don't know what to say. Andre, you got anything to say?"

Dad just mumbled, "There are no words for how I feel right now, Mom. My sons don't want to respect my authority. It looks like they'd rather raise themselves with no direction and no rules."

"I'm sorry, Dad. We can take it," I said, thinking that punishment would be better than him sounding like he just didn't care.

I'd never known him to use the silent treatment on us before. He must have been really hurt that we could let him down like this. Taking that trip just wasn't worth it. We should have done what he said. If we were ever gonna make him proud, then we were gonna have to do much better than this.

● ● ●

You'd better watch your back.

Those were the words I read on a piece of paper laying on my desk. Back at school on Monday morning, I looked around the classroom, wondering who would have left such a note.

At the time, I was the only one in the room. Since I rode with my dad and he had to be at school early, I was usually the first to arrive in the mornings. Someone must have placed it there on Friday before we went home.

My hunch told me that it had to be Tyrod. He'd already warned me to watch myself. But his handwriting was very bad, and this note was written very neatly. Either he was faking Mr. Wade out into thinking his writing was bad, he had someone write it for him, or the note wasn't from him at all. Hmm.

I was only ten years old. No one should be threatening me in school. Maybe it was Gilmer. I'm sure he could tell from my attitude that I didn't like the way he had thrown me under the bus.

As I sat there thinking about it, Mr. Wade walked in the room. "Good morning, Alec. Hope you had a good weekend," he said.

I really didn't because I had done something that my dad told me not to do. And that alone made me feel five times worse than when I was four and I broke Mom's vase that her mom gave her. When I wanted to pay her back, she reminded me that I didn't have any money. And, even if I did, it was something that couldn't be replaced. I remember how she cried for the rest of the day. I haven't played in the living room ever since.

"Alec, I'm going to make some copies. You know, I sense you've been really trying lately. I've been watching you and want you to know that I'm proud of how you're behaving. If I'm not back in time, you can do me a favor when the students arrive. Please tell your classmates to turn to page 59 in their grammar books and work on sentence fragments."

"But we haven't gone over that yet, sir," I said.

"I know. I just want to see how you guys do first. Then we'll go over it together when I get back. Hopefully, there won't be anyone else using the photocopier, and it won't take me a long time. Can you handle that?"

"Yes, sir."

Before Mr. Wade left the room, Gilmer came in, and I asked him, "Can I talk to you?"

"Didn't I just hear the teacher say something about starting on an assignment?" Gilmer asked, avoiding the question.

"Yeah, but the class isn't here yet. Besides, the bell hasn't rung. We have plenty of time. I just need to ask you something."

"Okay."

"You didn't leave me any strange notes or anything like that, did you?"

Gilmer looked at me like I was accusing him when all I did was ask a question. "No. What strange notes?"

"Nothing. Just forget it."

"Why do you think I would leave you a note? We don't even talk," he turned away from me and headed to his seat.

Annoyed, I touched his shoulder so he'd turn back to

face me. "You know what? I do wanna talk to you. I put my neck out for you. I was ready to help you when Tyrod and his buddies were giving you a hard time. You didn't even back me up with my dad. I don't understand."

"What don't you understand? I didn't ask for your help, okay?" he said, acting as if he wanted me to leave him alone.

Okay, so he didn't ask for my help. He was right. I had just learned the hard way that I needed to mind my own business.

A couple of minutes later, Tyrod walked into the classroom. He had a smug look on his face like he wanted me to say something about the note. But I wasn't going to give him the satisfaction. I stayed in my seat and waited until the rest of the students came in. Then I repeated what the teacher said about the assignment.

About fifteen minutes later, Mr. Wade returned. "Okay, class, put down your pencils and let's go over sentence fragments. Number one: 'The cake in the mixing bowl.'"

Morgan raised her hand. "It's a fragment."

"And why do you say that?" asked Mr. Wade.

"We don't know anything about the cake in the mixing bowl. It's missing a subject."

"Show off," Tyrod mumbled under his breath.

Mr. Wade said, "Very good, Morgan. Tyrod, do you have something you would like to say to the class?"

"No, sir."

"Okay then, you must be respectful or you'll be going to

the office. This is your last and final warning. Is that clear?"

"I got you, Mr. Wade. Be cool."

"Tyrod! Do you want me to send you to the office?"

"I want you to stop talkin'," Tyrod mumbled under his breath. "No, no, sir. I'll be good," he said, as Mr. Wade began walking toward him.

"You answer number two, Tyrod. The sentence is: 'Wait here.'"

"That's easy. That's a fragment."

"Incorrect. The subject is silent. It's understood that *you* are to wait here."

"That don't make no sense," Tyrod said, flipping his hand in the air.

"It's something you have to know."

Tyrod asked, "Well then, why couldn't *you* put the mix in the bowl?"

Mr. Wade said, "It's only in short command sentences that the pronoun *you* is understood. Now, number three: 'Red, yellow, blue, and green.' Alec?"

"Sir, that's a fragment because there is no predicate. We don't know what's going on with red, yellow, blue, and green because the fragment has no verb. The sentence could go: 'Red, yellow, blue, and green are cool colors.'"

"Good job. Number four: 'One, two, three, and four are my favorite numbers.' Trey?"

"That's a sentence. It has a subject and a predicate."

"Good. What's the subject?"

"Oh, come on, Mr. Wade. It's getting hard to tell."

"You can tell me. We talked about this."

"Well, 'one, two, three, and four' is a compound subject."

"Correct! Number five. Tyrod."

Tyrod grumbled, "You're callin' on me again?"

"Yes. 'Going to the store and going to the restaurant.' Is that a sentence or a fragment?"

"I don't know. That one's hard."

"You're not even trying," Trey spoke up and said.

Gilmer raised his hand. "That's a fragment."

"And why?"

"Because there's no subject. We don't know who's going to the store or the restaurant."

"Correct."

Then Mr. Wade walked down the aisle and looked at Tyrod's paper. He hadn't put down any of the answers for our assignment. What was going on with him?

"Tyrod, let's take your desk out into the hallway so you can finish your work while the rest of class goes over the answers. I'm not going to let you just sit here and write down the answers."

I was so glad that Mr. Wade took him out of the room. Not because he didn't know his work, but because he was such a troublemaker. The teacher was right, though. Why should he be given the answers when all the other classmates did the assignment? We were putting forth the effort, and he didn't do any of the work.

When Mr. Wade came back in, he reminded us, "Class,

you should all be familiar with the standard test, the CRCT. It's coming up soon, and you need to know everything we're going over. I know it's not counted for pass or fail for you fourth graders this year, but next year it will count. In DeKalb County, we have high expectations for you. If you don't do your best, then you won't pass the test."

"Oh, snap! Mr. Wade is rhyming," said Trey.

Mr. Wade gave Trey a look as if to say, *"Don't get the rest of the class started."*

"Students, every one of you has the ability to learn. You will succeed in learning if you are properly motivated to do so. It all comes from within. So, if you do your best, you will pass."

● ● ●

This Easter Sunday morning really brought a new meaning to me. I'm glad that I am a believer. And because I am, I know the Lord lives in me.

I don't always have nice thoughts, but God is working on me. For one thing, I really don't think too much of Tyrod because of the way he treats people. I'm not perfect, so I need God's grace to give me a caring heart.

On the way to church, I wanted to ask my dad a question. He still wasn't talking much to Antoine or me since we disobeyed him and tried to go to the store. It was worse than watching a movie on TV without being able to hear what anyone was saying.

So I've been thinking, *Dad just has to forgive us.* At the

least, I want him to forgive me. Antoine acted like he didn't care, but I definitely want to get back in Dad's good graces.

"I'm sorry," I spoke up and said. "I know I've been saying that all week, but I really am sorry, Dad."

I'm glad it was just the two of us. Antoine had gone to church with Grandma, Aunt Dot, and Lil P. That made it easier for Dad and me to speak freely and clear our minds.

"Alec, I know it feels like I'm being extra hard on you, but it's for your own good. Lately, I've been pulling away from you, but it's not because I don't love you or I don't care. I was very disappointed in you when you decided to go against what I told you not to do. Besides that, there's a lot going on at work . . . things going on with your mom . . . your grandmother's health is not so good. But, son, I'm still here . . . anything you need to talk to me about, just let me know. Please."

"Dad, did Jesus have to hang on a cross? I mean, I know we needed to be saved, but didn't it hurt?"

"I'm sure it hurt very much. They took nails and hammered them into His hands and feet. Do you remember the time when I was fixing one of the living room chairs for your mom and the nail accidentally flew across the room and stuck you in the foot?"

"Yeah. When a nail hit you, it made you yell out real loud. And you had to get three stitches because blood was gushing all over the place."

"Yes," Dad said with a laugh, "that's right. It might seem funny now, but it wasn't at the time. Even so, I still can't even imagine what it was like for Jesus to have nails driven through His hands and feet. Alec, to answer your question, He did it not only to save us but because He loves us and wants us to do better."

"I want to do better, Dad."

"Me too, son."

Later on in church, the pastor was talking about the same thing. He began by saying, "I've been thinking about all the suffering Jesus endured by hanging on the cross for you and for me. Jesus is the Son of God. He went through the pain of forgiving our sins and making it possible for us to live in heaven with Him when we die. Because He showed us His love by doing such a hard thing, we should show Him our love in return. The best way to do that is to follow His rules."

The pastor continued, "So, the way to live a better life is to obey God. Let me tell you the story about the first man, Adam, who disobeyed God. In the book of Genesis, God put Adam in a beautiful garden. He told Adam that he could eat from any tree that he wanted, except for one. Adam wasn't supposed to eat from the tree of the knowledge of good and evil. Then God gave Adam a wife to keep him company. Her name was Eve. Adam was supposed to care for her and teach Eve everything that God wanted them to do."

I was becoming more and more interested as the pastor told us more of the story: "One day, a snake came along. The snake was the enemy of God. So he was up to no good and wanted to turn Adam and Eve against God. This enemy, the snake, asked Eve why they couldn't eat from that one tree."

Then the pastor said these words to us: "People, know that God is our Protector, but we still have to be careful. Peer pressure is all around. Your enemy is anything or anybody that would take your attention away from God. When temptation comes, this is the thing to do. Pray to God for help and then obey what He tells you to do. Let your enemy know who has the upper hand."

Sometimes I don't understand the sermons. That's why I like Sunday school much better. It's easy to follow and easy to understand. But this time, I was getting every word and eating it up like a good meal!

I was learning that I had to do better because I believe in Jesus. I want to show Him that I love Him and I'm thankful for what He did for me. Even though Gilmer wasn't going to say thank you and Antoine didn't want to get along with me—I had be strong and stand tall.

Letter to Mom

Dear Mom,

Are you enjoying your new acting job? I really hope so because I want you to be happy. My friends can't wait to see the first show. They are really excited for you, and I know you'll be great too.

Mom, I enjoyed Easter Sunday and learned a good lesson about what Jesus wants us to do. He paid a big price for us because He loves us so much. Now, I really want to make Him proud of me. I want you and Dad to be proud of me too.

Your son,

Trying to be Good Alec

Word Search: HBCU Teams

HISTORICALLY BLACK COLLEGES AND UNIVERSITY TEAMS

There are four major HBCU athletic conferences. They are the Southern Intercollegiate Athletic Conference (SIAC), Mid-Eastern Athletic Conference (MEAC), Southwestern Athletic Conference (SWAC), and the Central Intercollegiate Athletic Association (CIAA). Below are some of the top schools that are great in the sport of basketball.

```
C  T  S  E  R  A  W  A  L  E  D  T
O  L  G  F  N  I  F  R  C  X  H  S
I  Z  E  M  Z  B  M  V  J  Q  O  N
C  H  V  V  A  N  K  I  E  N  O  I
N  G  B  S  E  A  P  R  Q  E  R  P
O  Z  D  E  A  L  D  G  J  T  A  P
T  H  U  I  Z  A  A  I  J  S  Y  O
P  F  N  N  S  C  M  N  R  X  G  C
M  S  K  A  R  O  L  I  D  O  O  I
A  F  Q  E  O  Y  U  A  Z  S  L  F
H  L  C  O  A  C  H  S  R  Q  T  F
U  B  B  A  Y  Q  K  T  Y  K  N  J
```

CLARK   **CLEVELANDST (Cleveland State)**

COPPINST (Coppin State)   **DELAWAREST (Delaware State)**

FLORIDAAM (Florida A&M)   **HAMPTON**   **VIRGINIAST (Virginia State)**

RIGHT
way

7

Man. I can't *believe Lil P. is here again,* I thought. Dad and I were pulling into our driveway after Easter service.

"Yes, I'm looking forward to a delicious dinner. This is a special day." Dad had a big smile on his face as he was talking to me. I just looked at him. He was thinking just the opposite of what I was thinking.

Dad went on talking. "Aunt Dot and Lil P. are going to have dinner with us. Isn't it great to see your cousin, Alec?"

I knew right then that we didn't agree. Whenever Lil P. came around, there was a different feeling in the air. He made Antoine turn into another person, and that wasn't cool. To keep from talking about how I really felt, I nodded. Dad wasn't ready to hear that I wasn't feelin' my cousin being there.

"Before we left for church this morning, your grand-mother told me what she was going to cook. We're having roast beef, macaroni and cheese, candied yams, and some fresh collard greens. Yes, sir! A meal fit for a king."

Dad could hardly finish parking the car before he said, "Come on, boy! Let's get out of this car right now. I can already taste it!"

As soon as we got inside, I knew he was right. I could smell the delicious food. Church had run a little long today because they were talking about next week's baptism service. So, like my father, I was ready to throw down and eat.

"Alec, go on in there and wash your hands. Tell Antoine and Lil P. to come with you," Grandma told me.

"Yes, ma'am."

As I passed Antoine's room, Lil P. was standing in the door, licking his lips. He looked at me like I was dinner. I knew he had trouble on his mind and couldn't wait to mess with me. Lil P. took one fist and shoved it into the palm of his hand, but I wasn't about to get beat up again. I walked right past him. If I didn't learn anything else from Trey and Gilmer, I learned that the only way to defeat a bully is to stand up to one. So I wasn't gonna let my cousin scare me.

Fifteen minutes later, we were all sitting at the table eating dinner. After Dad said a blessing over the food, he was the first one to talk about the spread on the table.

"Oh, you ladies really outdid yourselves . . . cabbage and dressing, too . . . with deviled eggs on the side. This meal really puts a smile on a guy's face. Right, boys?"

"And there's plenty of it too. Eat up and enjoy it," Grandma told Dad.

Lil P. made sure he sat next to me so he could kick me during the whole time we were eating. I hurried up and finished and then got up to rinse off my plate.

To avoid sitting back down again, I asked, "May I be excused?"

Dad said, "Everyone isn't done yet, son."

"I know, but I just wanna go outside and ride my bike for a bit."

"Okay, but what do you tell your grandma and Aunt Dot?"

"Thank you grandma and Aunt Dot," I said, as I walked around the table to kiss them both on the cheek.

As soon as I went outside, I headed straight to the garage. I don't know how he did it, but Lil P. surprised me. Somehow he beat me outside. Grabbing my handlebars, he said, "You didn't think you were comin' out here to play alone, did you?"

I tried to tug my bike away. "Get your hands off of my stuff."

"Or, what? Are you gonna go tell? Not if I'm makin' you hurt so bad that you won't be able to say anything."

"Leave him alone," Antoine called out from behind me.

I was shocked that my brother was standing there, ready to take up for me. Usually, he was right along with Lil P., making fun of me. Antoine came up to Lil P. and stood his ground.

"I said leave him alone," Antoine said to our cousin.

"You better stand back before I punch you too and hurt

your other arm. Plus, I don't get it. What's the big deal?"

Antoine put his hands over Lil P.'s mouth. I didn't know if he was doing that to keep him calm or to quiet him down from being too loud. Or, what? Was there something more to him wanting to keep Lil P. silent?

"You really better back off, Antoine, or I'm tellin' it all." Lil P.'s threat let me know that there was more.

"That's enough. It's over. Just leave him alone."

"You're the one who told me to mess him up," Lil P. yelled at Antoine. "Wanting me to beat and kick on him was all your idea."

"I know. But then I told you to squash it and leave him alone."

I couldn't believe what I was hearing. My brother told Lil P. to handle me? This was a nightmare. So frustrated, I tugged hard enough that I got my bike away from Lil P.'s grip and peddled away.

Don't cry, Alec. You don't need to cry. You can handle this, I thought, wiping away the tears that had already fallen.

I just prayed, *"Lord, this isn't right that my brother would sell me out. Yeah, we argue all the time, but I would never do something like that to him. Please tell me how I'm supposed to get over this. It hurts so much."*

Then I stopped my bike and jumped off. There was nowhere else to go, so I headed into the woods. I wasn't sure where I was going.

"Wait! Wait!" Antoine called out. I wasn't surprised that he had caught up to me. I knew from all the bike races we used to have that he could always beat me.

I ignored him and just kept walking. "Antoine, please leave me alone. I don't wanna hear anything you have to say."

"Alec, man, there are snakes out here in these woods."

"Okay, probably lions, tigers, and bears too. I'm not scared. Okay?"

He was tryin' hard to reason with me, but I wasn't tryin' to hear it. "Dad doesn't know where we are."

"He doesn't know that you told Lil P. to beat me up either."

Antoine tried to get closer to me, but I stepped away from him. I wanted to let him know how upset I was. I was in no mood to make up.

That's when he backed off a little and said, "I'm sorry, okay? I just got mad that day at the basketball tryouts. When I hit that guy, I couldn't believe you didn't side with me. Besides, I didn't really tell Lil P. to hurt you and stuff, I just told him that you needed to learn to stick by family. But, when that dude broke my arm, I learned a hard lesson. I promise I'll talk to Dad about what I did."

Then I started to believe him because he really did sound for real when he said, "You're already a Christian and I'm tryin' to learn about that. In church today, I was really listening when they were talkin' about Jesus being on the cross and everything. Man, it really got to me when I heard that Jesus asked His Father to forgive the people that hurt Him."

Antoine was quiet for a minute, before he said, "I guess I'm askin' for you to forgive me, Alec."

My brother hadn't sounded that serious in a long time. I prayed about it, and I guess this was my answer. Since I am a Christian, I had to do what Jesus would do—and that was to forgive. Antoine and I hugged. I could feel it in my heart that God was happy that we did.

● ● ●

I was so glad that the school year was about to be over. It had been a long year in the fourth grade. Mom being away, so much happened. The CRCT standard test was pretty hard, but I passed it. I even helped Antoine study for it, and he passed too.

Thinking about it all on this Monday morning, I couldn't help but smile. Now that it was almost time for a break. Of course, I was still gonna see Dad every day, but at least for a while it would only be at home. Two more weeks and counting. I couldn't wait.

I stepped into the boys' washroom for a quick second, and when I came out, I was really confused. I knew I had put my book bag down by the door, but it wasn't there anymore. I thought maybe somebody had picked it up, saw my name and my teacher's name, and returned it to Mr. Wade's classroom.

Thankfully, I had some time before the bell rang. I hadn't been tardy all year, and I wanted to keep it that way. On the way to my classroom, I looked in all the other fourth grade classrooms. My book bag was nowhere to be seen.

I scratched my head and thought, *I did leave it by the washroom door, right?* After replaying my exact steps three times, I turned the corner and there it was. To my surprise, Tyrod was kneeling down next to my book bag with his hand inside it.

"What are you doin'?" I yelled out.

"Here you go. I was just leavin' it right here," he said, holding my book back with a sly look on his face.

I snatched the paper he had in his other hand before he could drop it on the floor. It was a note that read: School's almost out and I'm going to get you, Alec. Watch yourself.

"You might as well go on and sign your name to it, Tyrod," I said to him.

"Why would I? I didn't write it."

Wanting to get back at him, I said, "You're right. Who-ever wrote this has good handwriting. You can't even spell, and all these words are spelled correctly. Besides, you're too much of a chicken to leave me a note like this. That's why you tried to make it seem like somebody else did it."

Tyrod couldn't stand the fact that I was making him look bad. So he just blurted out, "Okay, I did write it. I need to bring you down because you think you're all that. Yeah, I don't have the best writing and I can't spell so good, but I can do better when I want to. I was the smartest one in my class last year. Now you and Morgan are tryin' to show me up."

"Even though it didn't look like you wrote the note, I saw you puttin' it in my book bag. So, thanks for tellin' me."

"Yeah, I wrote it. So what?"

"I'm goin' to the office, and I'm tellin' my dad. That's what."

"Yeah. Like he's gonna believe you. Ha ha ha. He didn't believe you last time, and he's not gonna believe you now. My mom is just waitin' to come up here and tell him a thing or two."

I froze in my tracks. Tyrod was right. What made me really believe that my dad was going to believe me now? What would make him do the right thing this time and punish Tyrod?

"Yeah. I can see it all over your face. You don't even believe it yourself that your dad's got your back. What you gonna do now?"

I hung my head low until a voice from behind me said, "It's not that I don't believe my son, Tyrod. I just needed proof. I've watched you all school year. You've been getting failing grades, bullying people, and giving your teachers a hard time. That's why I called a conference with your mother today. She and I were headed to get you."

We both looked up and a lady was coming around the corner. Tyrod's mom just looked at her son with disappointment all over her face.

"Tyrod, I can't wait to get you home. You turn around and apologize to this young man right now. I can't believe you thought I would put up with this kind of behavior. Threatening someone? Tyrod, what's going on with you? I know it's been hard since your father left home, but acting out isn't the right way to be. You have to accept that he has a new family. We're going to be okay."

"Alec, son. Why don't you go back to class," Dad said to me.

Tyrod's mom added, "No, sir, not until my son apologizes."

"Sorry," Tyrod said to me, as he stared at the floor.

Listening to everything his mother just said made me feel so bad for him. I mean, my mom was gone too, but she didn't have another family. I could only imagine how he was hurting. But that still didn't make it right for him to be so mean. I know for myself that it doesn't pay to be mad all the time.

Putting myself in his shoes, I reached out my hand for Tyrod to shake it. "It's okay, man."

"For real, it's all right?" he said, as his mother stood next to him and smiled.

"Yeah," I replied, as I watched the two of them and my dad walk on to his office.

I picked up my book bag, and as I headed to my class, Gilmer stopped me. "Hey, can I talk to you?" he asked me. "I need to tell you something. I want to say thanks for taking up for me earlier this year. Lately, I've been thinking about it all. I should have thanked you in the first place. Who knows what would have happened if you hadn't stepped in? It was me against five other guys, and that was too much. When I left school that day, I didn't get hurt because you stepped up. I should have spoken up in your dad's office."

I stood there listening to Gilmer explain himself. Finally, he was opening up to someone. It really made me understand him when he said, "Now, don't get me wrong. I really like being by myself, so I'm not looking for any buddies or anything. But I realize that you've gotta let people know when they do good things for you. You're a real role model. Keep on showing everybody how things are supposed to be done, Alec."

● ● ●

"Thanks for inviting me and my family to the preview of your mom's show. It was so good," Morgan said to me, smiling and acting happy.

"You wanna talk to her?" I asked Morgan.

"With all of those reporters around her, she's not gonna want to talk to me," she replied.

"Well, I want to get her autograph," Trey jumped in. He already had his pen and program ready.

I walked over to Mom with my two friends. She must have seen me coming because the reporters walked off. Maybe she told them to come back later. That made me feel real special because it showed that she put me above everyone else around her. But Mom had done a great job on her show. She deserved all of the attention she was getting.

"So, who do we have here?" Mom said, with a big smile. "Miss Morgan, I haven't seen you since Thanksgiving dinner."

"Yes, ma'am. You were so great tonight! My grandparents keep asking me what I want to be when I grow up. After seeing you, I think I want to be an actress."

"Just keep working hard in school, and everything will pay off. Okay?"

Morgan nodded.

"Mom, this is Trey," I said to her.

"I don't think I've met Trey before," she said, before turning to my friend. "But I've heard a lot about you. Thanks for being a very good buddy to my son," Mom told him.

"Lisa, I'm sorry to interrupt you with your kids, but they need a few more minutes of your time," the producer of the show spoke up as he pointed toward the reporters. It was Mom's buddy, Mr. Kim Fox. The one I met in California.

As a reminder, I nudged Trey in the arm. I didn't want him to forget about his autograph.

"Oh, could you please sign this first, Mrs. London?" Trey asked her.

"I sure can, come on and walk this way with me," Mom said, taking Trey's pen and program.

Before walking off, she said, "Morgan, it was nice seeing you again. Alec, tell your dad that I'll be done in a minute."

"Well, I gotta go. Thanks again for inviting me, Alec,"

Morgan said, as her stepdad waved his hand for her to join their family.

I was left standing there alone with Mr. Fox. "Alec, I want you to know that your mom loves you and your family. You should be very proud of her. I want to reassure you that your mom and I are just good friends. I apologize if I led you to believe anything more. I really respect her. As soon as she's done with these last reporters, she's all yours." He stuck out his hand, and I shook it.

"Is everything okay over here?" Dad walked up and asked.

Mr. Fox replied, "Yes. I was just telling your son that his mom will be ready to go in a few minutes."

"Oh, okay. Congratulations, man. The show was real nice," Dad said.

"We're hoping to get some good ratings when it hits the air next week."

"You will, for sure."

Just then Mom joined us. "Okay, I'm ready to go now. Where's Antoine?"

"He's over there by the food table," I pointed out.

"I'm going that way. I'll tell him you're ready to leave," Mr. Fox said. Then he turned back to Dad and surprised me when he said, "Dr. London, you have a very lovely family."

Dad put his arm around Mom and kissed her on the cheek. "Thanks, I know I'm a blessed man."

I really liked seeing my parents so happy. As we followed Mom into her dressing room to get her things, I prayed, *"Lord, I really want my family to be happy always. They seem happy now. Dad has a job, and Mom is doing her acting thing. You're blessing us, but is it for real? Or, are they acting?"*

"Alec, what are you thinking about?" Dad asked me, interrupting my prayer.

"I was praying for you and Mom. Are you guys really over what was bothering you before? And, Mom, you did your TV episodes. Are you coming back home now?"

"Alec, not tonight, honey," Mom said. Letting me know that this wasn't the time, she pinched my cheek.

"Is it really such a crime to want my family together and everything to be okay? I don't know what's going on, that's why I'm asking you guys. I wanna know. That's why I prayed to God, Dad. I don't know what else to do."

"Son, you have to trust God and wait on Him. His ways are higher than our ways. Don't worry. It'll all be okay. No matter what happens, we'll always have your and your brother's interests in mind."

Mom could tell by the look on my face that I still wasn't sure, so she told me, "We're not trying to confuse you, Alec, but there are certain things that adults have to work out. I guess we're saying to bear with us and let God be in control."

"That's right. Just remember that God is always with us. Now, let's take your mom out so we can celebrate."

Antoine was right on time when he ran into the room. Lightening the mood, he said, "Mom, you were so good!

Wasn't she, Alec?" With whipped cream all over his face, he apologized. "I'm sorry, Mom. But those little cakes with the strawberries on them are so delicious!"

Mom just smiled at Antoine and put her arm around his shoulder as they walked out together.

Dad asked me, "Are you okay, Alec?"

"Yeah. I guess it's like Grandma says, 'God may not come when you want Him to, but He'll be there right on time.'"

"Exactly. Tonight has been amazing, so let's just enjoy it. Don't focus so much on tomorrow. Let God take care of it."

As Dad put his arm around me, we walked over to the front door where Mom and Antoine were waiting for us. All of a sudden, it just hit me that I was a really blessed kid. I was learning that you can't do anything you want any old time you want. There are rules that you have to follow and adults that you always have to listen to. There's no need to worry or fear because when God has your life in the palm of His hand—you're as safe as anyone can be.

Now I really want to learn how to trust the Lord every day. I'm only ten, and I have a lot of living to do. Right now, I don't know if I want to be a doctor or a lawyer. I don't even know if I want pancakes or waffles in the morning.

But I do know that, day by day, I'm going to follow Jesus and do what He wants me to do. And if I can do that, then I'll be okay—because in God's eyes—that's the right way.

Letter to Mom

Dear Mom,

It's been quite a time of learning for me. Looking back, I think I've grown a lot over this past year because I'm beginning to learn the rules. Through all the drama with Antoine, Lil P., Tyrod, and Gilmer, I know how to be strong and stand up for myself now. From now on, I won't run from trouble, but I'll always try to do the right thing.

I'm also learning how to trust God that everything is going to work out between you and Dad. I really want us to be a strong family. And I know that the most important thing is that we must all obey God's number one rule. It doesn't matter what we must face in life, we can be champions if we always show each other love.

Most of all, I know that God loves us all, and His love is strong enough to keep us together.

Your son,
Trying to be Right Alec

Word Search: Famous Basketball Players

In 1950, Earl Lloyd, Chuck Cooper, and Nat "Sweetwater" Clifton entered the NBA and became pioneers for today's great African-American basketball players. Find the names of other great players who have followed in their path.

```
O  N  Z  T  J  J  C  L  O  C  K  S
A  W  P  E  P  A  R  K  S  L  V  J
C  C  H  D  I  K  S  N  A  Q  T  O
P  H  W  A  P  A  C  E  K  Q  K  I
A  U  A  W  F  J  N  Q  I  V  O  N
S  S  J  M  O  O  E  S  R  P  W  J
S  P  E  R  B  T  N  A  Y  R  B  O
E  X  D  M  M  E  Y  N  P  O  A  H
R  A  T  M  A  Y  R  B  X  S  I  N
N  J  D  Z  Q  J  S  L  I  B  L  S
D  J  T  F  R  E  E  T  I  B  Z  O
K  T  V  T  H  R  O  W  E  N  L  N
```

BRYANT (Kobe)   CHAMBERLIN (Wilt)   JAMES (LeBron)

JOHNSON (Magic)   JORDAN (Michael)   ONEAL (Shaquille)

WADE (Dwayne)

LEARNING THE RULES

Stephanie Perry Moore & Derrick Moore
Discussion Questions

1. Alec London learns his mother isn't staying in Georgia. Even though she is doing what she feels is best, do you think Alec should be sad? How do you react when your parents do something you don't agree with?

2. Antoine and Alec go to basketball practice, and Antoine whacks his teammate in the scrimmage. Do you think Alec should have told the coach that he saw his brother being too physical? Do you stand up for what is right even if it's tough to do so?

3. Alec's cousin Lil P. comes over to play and bullies him. Do you think Alec was right in not telling an adult? What is the best way to handle someone that is bullying you?

4. Gilmer is on the playground, and Tyrod surrounds him with some of his buddies, and Trey wants Alec to do something. Do you feel Alec should get involved? When someone else is being bullied, what is the best thing to do?

5. When Antoine plays a rough basketball team, the boys hurt his arm. Do you think that helped Antoine learn not to be mean to others? What does the saying, "What goes around comes around mean"?

6. When Alec goes to church, he learns about the story of Adam and Eve. Do you think Alec understood what he learned? What did you learn about the fall of mankind from that story?

7. Lil P. gets in Alec's face and Antoine takes on his cousin, telling him to leave his brother alone. Do you feel Alec needed to forgive his brother for being a part of his cousin bullying him in the first place? How can your relationship with your siblings/cousins be a good one when they hurt you?

Order of Sentences

Instructions: Use the paragraphs below to place the sentences in the correct order.

Example: (1) Alec passed the language arts test. (2) Alec studied really hard. (3) Mr. Wade told the class they were going to have a big exam on what they had learned. (4) Mr. Wade taught the class about similes.
Answer: 4, 3, 2, 1

(1) The family ate a delicious meal. (2) Alec went with his grandmother to the grocery store. (3) They bought chicken, rice, and green beans. (4) Alec helped his grandmother prepare dinner.

_____

(2) Alec and his team got dressed for the basketball game when they got to the gym. (2) They won the game. (3) His team warmed up before the start of the game. (4) Alec's team outscored the other team.

_____

(3) Alec was not happy. (2) Antione poured wet noodles on Alec. (3) Antione played a prank on Alec. (4) When Alec looked in the mirror, he laughed because it was funny.

_____

(4) He told his father that his shoes did not fit. (2) Alec loved his new kicks. (3) They went to the mall to get him a new pair. (4) Alec's tennis shoes were too small.

_____

(5) Alec agreed to play. (2) Trey and Billy asked Alec to play kickball. (3) They asked Morgan and other girls to play so they would have a team to play against. (4) The girls won by a landslide.

_____

Decimal Computations

Instructions: Find the answers to the following addition and subtraction number sentences.

Example: $6.1 + 5.2 = \_\_\_\_$; Answer is 11.3

$6.8 - 5.1 = \_\_\_\_$; Answer is 1.7

1) $4.3 + 6.3 = \_\_\_\_$ 2) $5.5 - 2.3 = \_\_\_\_$

3) $2.4 + 5.3 = \_\_\_\_$ 4) $9.6 - 3.3 = \_\_\_\_$

5) $7.5 + 2.4 = \_\_\_\_$ 6) $6.7 - 4.6 = \_\_\_\_$

7) $5.1 + 8.2 = \_\_\_\_$ 8) $8.8 - 7.2 = \_\_\_\_$

9) $4.9 + 3.0 = \_\_\_\_$ 10) $6.9 - 5.4 = \_\_\_\_$

11) $0.24 + 0.25 = \_\_\_\_$ 12) $0.68 - 0.32 = \_\_\_\_$

13) $0.71 + 0.23 = \_\_\_\_$ 14) $0.97 - 0.65 = \_\_\_\_$

15) $0.34 + 0.55 = \_\_\_\_$ 16) $0.72 - 0.51 = \_\_\_\_$

17 $0.16 + 0.81 = \_\_\_\_$ 18) $0.86 - 0.32 = \_\_\_\_$

19) $5.44 + 3.52 = \_\_\_\_$ 20) $8.37 - 6.25 = \_\_\_\_$

Teach Me, Coach: Basketball

Oh, so you can hoop, huh? Well, you must have more than skills to play basketball, you also must learn the rules. So here are the basics. Basketball is a really enjoyable game, but to make the sport fair and fun, everyone on the court must comply with the rules and regulations. There are lots of dos and don'ts. We will go over the essentials of the game, including the court, players, offense, defense, and fouls.

Basketball Court

The game is played on a rectangular floor called the court. The court's length is 94 feet. The basketball game starts with a jump ball in the center of the court. The referee blows the whistle, and two players, one from each team, jump up to swat the ball to their teammates. There are baskets/hoops on each end of the court. How long is the basketball court? _____

Scoring

There are basically three different types of points to make in the game of basketball. Two points can be scored if a player makes a basket inside the three-point shot line. Three points can be scored if the basket is from behind the three-point line. One point can be scored if a foul shot is made. How many points are made from one foul shot? _____

Game format

Basketball is a timed sport. Each game is divided into sections. All levels have two halves. On the professional level, quarters are twelve minutes long. On the college level, each half is twenty minutes long. On the high school and below, the halves are divided into eight- (and sometimes, six-) minute quarters. There is a halftime between halves. If the score is tied at the end of regulation, then overtime periods of various lengths are played until a team wins the game. Each team has a basket to defend. The other basket is their scoring basket. The teams switch baskets at halftime. How long is a quarter on the professional level? _____

Basketball Players

The rules in basketball allow each team to have 5 players on the court at a time, 10 players from both teams. Teams are allowed to substitute players between plays. Each team must start a play from outside of the court lines. The five positions on the team are: 1 center, 2 guards, and 2 forwards. All 5 players have to play defense as well. How many players from one team are on the court at one time? _____

The Basketball Play

The team that wins the tip-off gets the ball first and tries to make a basket. The ball is moved up and down the court toward the basket by passing or dribbling. When a team makes a basket, the ball goes to the other team. The team with the ball is called the offense. The team without the ball is called the defense. Defense tries to steal the ball, contest shots, steal and deflect passes, and go for rebounds. If a team wins the tip-off do they get the ball first? _____

Basketball Fouls and Violations

There are several penalties in basketball that result in the other team getting to make a foul shot. They are charging, blocking, flagrant foul, intentional foul, and technical foul. When a violation occurs, the team that commits the violation loses the ball. Violations are walking/traveling, carrying/palming, double dribbling, holding the ball, goaltending, backcourt violation, and time restrictions. A penalty results in what type of shot? _____

Teach Me, Coach

Learning the rules of basketball can make this game a fantastic sport. Always remember that the game is a team sport and should be played fairly. Always listen to your coach, work hard in practice, and during the game, give it your all. Know that basketball is exciting and that you're flying when you jump to make a basket. So have fun and make some baskets!

Chapter 1 Solution

FREETHROW (Free Throw)   **JERSEY**   **JUMPBALL (Jump Ball)**

PASS   **SLAMDUNK (Slam Dunk)**

SNEAKERS   **THREEPTSHOT (Three-Point Shot)**

Chapter 2 Solution

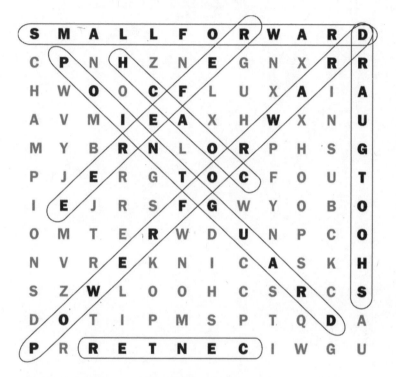

CENTER   COACH   POINTGUARD (Point Guard)
POWERFORWARD (Power Forward)   REFEREE
SHOOTGUARD (Shooting Guard)   SMALLFORWARD (Small Forward)

Chapter 3 Solution

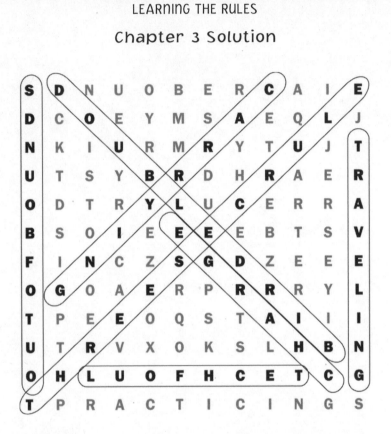

S	D	N	U	O	B	E	R	C	A	I	E
D	C	O	E	Y	M	S	A	E	Q	L	J
N	K	I	U	R	M	R	Y	T	U	J	T
U	T	S	Y	B	R	D	H	R	A	E	R
O	D	T	R	Y	L	U	C	E	R	R	A
B	S	O	I	E	E	E	E	B	T	S	V
F	I	N	C	Z	S	G	D	Z	E	E	E
O	G	O	A	E	R	P	R	R	R	Y	L
T	P	E	E	O	Q	S	T	A	I	I	I
U	T	R	V	X	O	K	S	L	H	B	N
O	H	L	U	O	F	H	C	E	T	C	G
T	P	R	A	C	T	I	C	I	N	G	S

CARRYING   **CHARGE**   **DOUBLEDRIB** (Double Dribble)
OUTOFBOUNDS (Out of Bounds)   **TECHFOUL** (Technical Foul)
THREESECRULE (Three-Second Rule)   **TRAVELING**

Chapter 4 Solution

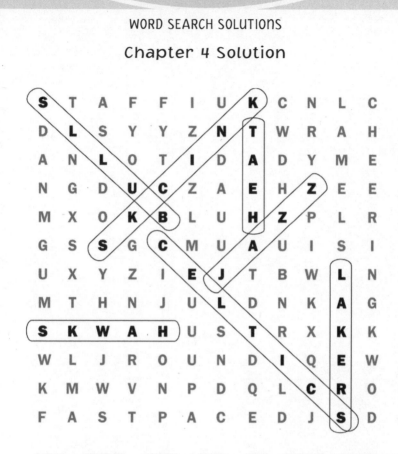

BULLS   CELTICS   HAWKS   HEAT   JAZZ   KNICKS   LAKERS

Chapter 5 Solution

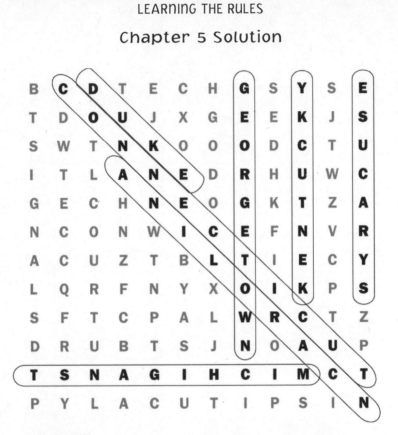

B	C	D	T	E	C	H	G	S	Y	S	E
T	D	O	U	J	X	G	E	E	K	J	S
S	W	T	N	K	O	O	O	D	C	T	U
I	T	L	A	N	E	D	R	H	U	W	C
G	E	C	H	N	E	O	G	K	T	Z	A
N	C	O	N	W	I	C	E	F	N	V	R
A	C	U	Z	T	B	L	T	I	E	C	Y
L	Q	R	F	N	Y	X	O	I	K	P	S
S	F	T	C	P	A	L	W	R	C	T	Z
D	R	U	B	T	S	J	N	O	A	U	P
T	S	N	A	G	I	H	C	I	M	C	T
P	Y	L	A	C	U	T	I	P	S	I	N

CONNECTICUT   DUKE   GEORGETOWN   KENTUCKY
MICHIGANST (Michigan State)   NCAROLINA (North Carolina)
SYRACUSE

Chapter 6 Solution

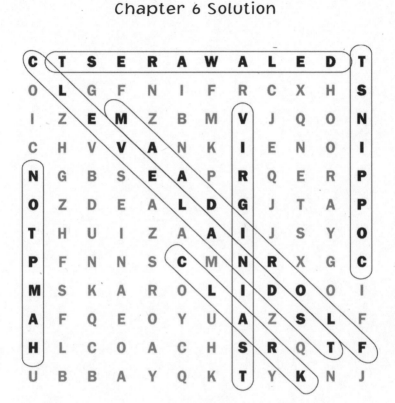

CLARK

CLEVELANDST (Cleveland State)

COPPINST (Coppin State)

DELAWAREST (Delaware State)

FLORIDAAM (Florida A&M)

HAMPTON   **VIRGINIAST (Virginia State)**

Chapter 7 Solution

O	N	Z	T	J	J	C	L	O	C	K	S
A	W	P	E	P	A	R	K	S	L	V	J
C	C	H	D	I	K	S	N	A	Q	T	O
P	H	W	A	P	A	C	E	K	Q	K	I
A	U	A	W	F	J	N	Q	I	V	O	N
S	S	J	M	O	O	E	S	R	P	W	J
S	P	E	R	B	T	N	A	Y	R	B	O
E	X	D	M	M	E	Y	N	P	O	A	H
R	A	T	M	A	Y	R	B	X	S	I	N
N	J	D	Z	Q	J	S	L	I	B	L	S
D	J	T	F	R	E	E	T	I	B	Z	O
K	T	V	T	H	R	O	W	E	N	L	N

BRYANT (Kobe)   **CHAMBERLIN (Wilt)**   **JAMES (LeBron)**

JOHNSON (Magic)   **JORDAN (Michael)**   **ONEAL (Shaquille)**

WADE (Dwayne)

Answer Keys

Order of Sentences

1) 2, 3, 4, 1
2) 1, 3, 4, 2
3) 3, 2, 1, 4
4) 4, 1, 3, 2
5) 2, 1, 3, 4

Decimal Computations

1) 10.6
2) 3.2
3) 7.7
4) 6.3
5) 9.9
6) 2.1
7) 13.3
8) 1.6
9) 7.9
10) 1.5
11) 0.49
12) 0.36
13) 0.94
14) 0.32
15) 0.89
16) 0.21
17) 0.97
18) 0.54
19) 8.96
20) 2.12

ACKNOWLEDGMENTS

We love family game night. In the Moore home we play Monopoly, Chinese checkers, Taboo, Scattergories, Apples to Apples, and Sequence. However, the only way we can have amazing fun is if we learn the true rules of each game and play by them. Life is similar to board games. There are rules, guidelines, and laws that must be followed. When you honor your mother and father, do what your teachers tell you, and obey the Bible, you can succeed and fly. And we pray this novel helps every reader.

We have a lot of people to thank. Especially our dear friends Antonio and Gloria London and family who inspired us with the character's last name. Also . . .

For our parents, Dr. Franklin and Shirley Perry, and Ann Redding, we have learned so much from you. Thank you for always being there.

For our Moody/Lift Every Voice Books team, especially, Greg Thornton, we have learned what being a class act in business is from you. Thank you for leading God's way and developing an imprint to speak to the African-American market.

For our Georiga Tech Fellowship of Christian Athletes supporters, especially Peyton Day and Jim and Deen Sanders. From you we have learned what true sowing is all about. Thank you for allowing your financial gifts to help us minister to student athletes.

For our assistants, Ciara Roundtree and Alyxandra Pinkston, we learned there are college students ready to take their game to the next level. Thank you for being responsible.

For our friends who are dear to our hearts, Calvin Johnson, Tashard Choice, Chett and Lakeba Williams, Dennis and Leslie Perry, Clayton and Kelly Ivey, Jay and Debbie Spencer, Randy Roberts, John Rainey, Peyton Day, Jim and Deen Sanders, Paul and Susan Johnson, Bobby and Sarah Lundy, Sid Callaway, Dicky Clark, Danny Buggs, Chan and Laurie Gailey, Patrick and Krista Nix, Byron and Kim Johnson, Jenell Clark, Carol Hardy, Nicole Smith, Jackie Dixon, Harry and Torian Colon, Byron and Kim Forest, Vickie Davis, Brock White, Jamell Meeks, Michele Jenkins, Christine Nixon, Lois Barney, Veronica Evans, Sophia Nelson, Laurie Weaver, Byrant and Taiwanna Brown-Bolds, Deborah Thomas, Yolanda Rodgers-Howsie, Dayna Fleming, Denise Gilmore, Thelma Day, Adrian Davis, and Donald and Deborah Bradley, we learned the meaning of friendship from you. We are thankful to have you in our lives.

ACKNOWLEDGMENTS

For our son, Dustyn, and youngest daughter, Sheldyn, we learn daily what it means to care for others more than you care for yourself by being the best parents we can be. We are thankful for these K–12 school years we have with you.

For our new young readers, we are learning that each of you can be all you want to be as you take in the lessons of this book. We are thankful this book is available to help you on your journey.

And for our Savior, we still have much to learn from You. However, we are so thankful You left the Holy Spirit to dwell within us and comfort us.

MAKING THE TEAM

The Alec London books are chapter books written for boys, 8–12 years old. Alec London is introduced in Stephanie Perry Moore's previously released series, Morgan Love. In this new series, readers get a glimpse of Alec's life up close and personal. The series provides moral lessons that will aid in character development, teaching boys how to effectively deal with the various issues they face at this stage of life. The books will also help boys develop their English and math skills as they read through the stories and complete the entertaining and educational exercises provided at the end of each chapter and in the back of the book.

OTHER BOOKS IN THE SERIES:

Also available as eBooks

LEARNING THE RULES
GOING THE DISTANCE
WINNING THE BATTLE
TAKING THE LEAD

L E V B
LIFT EVERY VOICE BOOKS

LiftEveryVoiceBooks.com
MoodyPublishers.com

ALSO RANS SERIES

The Also Rans series is written for boys, ages 8–12. This series enourages youth, especially young boys, to give all they've got in everything they do and never give up.

978-0-8024-2253-8

RUN, JEREMIAH, RUN

As a foster child, life for Jeremiah is a garbage bag filled with his things, a new school, and worst of all, finding a new family. Jeremiah holds on to his grandmother's promise of a handful of mustard seeds being planted one day to grow into a tree of his own. After being expelled from school again, he thinks that no one will want him to be a part of their family. With the help of his friends, he learns about teamwork and what it means to persevere.

978-0-8024-2259-0

COMING ACROSS JORDAN

When Jordan and her brother Kevin decide to paint a mural (which is really graffiti) on the school's property, they get in trouble. They learn along with their good friend, Melanie, the lesson that even in using their talents to do something good, they have to pay attention and not break the rules.

Also available as eBooks

L E V B
LIFT EVERY VOICE BOOKS

LiftEveryVoiceBooks.com
MoodyPublishers.com

MORGAN LOVE SERIES

978-0-8024-2263-7

978-0-8024-2264-4

978-0-8024-2267-5   978-0-8024-2266-8   978-0-8024-2265-1

The Morgan Love series is a chapter book series written for girls, 7–9 years old. The books provide moral lessons that will aid in character develop-ment. They will also help young girls develop their vocabulary, English, and math skills as they read through the stories and complete the enter-taining and educational exercises provided at the end of each chapter and in the back of the book.

Also available as
eBooks

L E V B
LIFT EVERY VOICE BOOKS

LiftEveryVoiceBooks.com
MoodyPublishers.com